Praise for Meagan McKinney
from *Romantic Times:*

On ONE SMALL SECRET
(Silhouette Desire #1222):

"Ms. McKinney's vividly depicted characters
will win your heart."

On THE COWBOY MEETS HIS MATCH
(Silhouette Desire #1299):

"Meagan McKinney sets off plenty of fireworks
for her readers."

On THE M.D. COURTS HIS NURSE
(Silhouette Desire #1354):

"Ms. McKinney's
THE M.D. COURTS HIS NURSE is a lively tale
with some highly charged scenes, snappy
dialogue and lovable characters."

* * *

Don't miss BILLIONAIRE BOSS,
the latest book from Meagan McKinney
in her engaging series

MATCHED IN MONTANA

*Wedding bells always ring
when this town matriarch plays Cupid.*

Dear Reader,

Spring into the new season with six fresh passionate, powerful and provocative love stories from Silhouette Desire.

Experience first love with a young nurse and the arrogant surgeon who stole her innocence, in *USA TODAY* bestselling author Elizabeth Bevarly's *Taming the Beastly MD* (#1501), the latest title in the riveting DYNASTIES: THE BARONES continuity series. Another *USA TODAY* bestselling author, Cait London, offers a second title in her HEARTBREAKERS miniseries—*Instinctive Male* (#1502) is the story of a vulnerable heiress who finds love in the arms of an autocratic tycoon.

And don't miss RITA® Award winner Marie Ferrarella's *A Bachelor and a Baby* (#1503), the second book of Silhouette's crossline series THE MOM SQUAD, featuring single mothers who find true love. In *Tycoon for Auction* (#1504) by Katherine Garbera, a lady executive wins the services of a commitment-shy bachelor. A playboy falls in love with his secretary in *Billionaire Boss* (#1505) by Meagan McKinney, the latest MATCHED IN MONTANA title. And a Native American hero's fling with a summer-school teacher produces unexpected complications in *Warrior in Her Bed* (#1506) by Cathleen Galitz.

This April, shower yourself with all six of these moving and sensual new love stories from Silhouette Desire.

Enjoy!

Joan Marlow Golan

Joan Marlow Golan
Senior Editor, Silhouette Desire

Please address questions and book requests to:
Silhouette Reader Service
U.S.: 3010 Walden Ave., P.O. Box 1325, Buffalo, NY 14269
Canadian: P.O. Box 609, Fort Erie, Ont. L2A 5X3

Billionaire
Boss

MEAGAN McKINNEY

Published by Silhouette Books
America's Publisher of Contemporary Romance

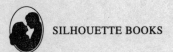

SILHOUETTE BOOKS

ISBN 0-373-76505-3

BILLIONAIRE BOSS

Visit Silhouette at www.eHarlequin.com

Printed in U.S.A.

Books by Meagan McKinney

Silhouette Desire

One Small Secret #1222
*The Cowboy Meets His Match #1299
*The M.D. Courts His Nurse #1354
*Plain Jane & the Hotshot #1493
*The Cowboy Claims His Lady #1499
*Billionaire Boss #1505

Silhouette Intimate Moments

*The Lawman Meets His Bride #1037

*Matched in Montana

MEAGAN McKINNEY

is the author of over a dozen novels—hardcover and paperback historical and contemporary women's fiction. In addition to romance, she likes to inject mystery and thriller elements into her work. Currently she lives in the Garden District of New Orleans with her two young sons, two very self-entitled cats and a crazy red mutt. Her favorite hobbies are traveling to the Arctic and, of course, reading!

One

"**M**s. Meadows, he'll see you now," announced the autocratic voice of the executive secretary.

Kirsten Meadows stood, already feeling like the poor relation next to the chic older woman. She herself wore a black suit from the local mall and a string of fake pearls. There was no competing with the executive secretary's costly designer outfit, but as Kirsten always did, she hid her fear and worries behind a placid expression.

Certainly, on the brighter side, she told herself, the secretary must be well paid to afford such an expensively tailored suit. The job of personal assistant to the boss would be, too.

With that giving her courage, she stepped into the office of the rich and powerful Seth Morgan.

Her bravado abandoned her at the polished mahogany door.

The man didn't greet her; he didn't even look up from his desk. His precisely clipped dark hair and stern chiseled face belied the fact that he was only thirty-three, not even six years older than Kirsten.

She surmised that the stressful lifestyle of the wealthy financier was what put the scowl on his face, even as she prayed it wasn't her résumé that he was reading. It had taken her last dime to fly to Manhattan to interview. If she didn't get the job, she was sunk.

"I've seen better." Seth Morgan finally looked up.

Kirsten was pinned by an icy stare. "Are you speaking of my résumé?" she finally asked, feeling foolish beneath the man's piercing stare.

He nodded and leaned back in his black leather chair to study her.

The Italian suit he wore fit so well it didn't even crease. His tie was ice-blue and only added to the coldness of his expression.

"Fluent in five languages, the daughter of a

career diplomat—it could be anyone.'' He snapped the résumé with his forefinger and then stared at her, almost as if he was daring her to refute his summation.

Kirsten refrained from releasing a defeated sigh. There was no way this arrogant rich man was going to see her beg. He'd done her a terrible disservice by requesting her to come to New York, but if the trip had been a failure, she sure wasn't going to give him, the Wall Street marauder that he was, the satisfaction of knowing that he'd ruined her.

Quietly she lifted her head and stared back.

''I'm sorry if you don't feel I'm qualified,'' she began. ''However, you had my résumé before you asked for an interview. You certainly could have turned me down in a letter without my having to come all the way to Manhattan from Montana. You've wasted all of our time—''

''Why should I give you the job?''

His words came like a gunshot.

Casually he braced his fingers together in a V and perused her.

Against her will she begrudgingly decided he had nice hands, strong and not paper-pusher pale. They suited his harshly handsome face.

Steeling herself in order to draw on her last

reserves, she said, "I could do very well for your estate in Mystery, Montana, because I know it as well as anyone. Yes, my father served as chargé d'affaires for several ambassadors, but every summer, Mother took me back to her birthplace, and after the divorce—"

She paused, still wounded by the memories more than a decade old of costly divorce-court battles her father had waged on her mother. The final cruelty was her mother's impoverished lifestyle after the wealth of an expatriate. The injustice of it had kept Kirsten and her sister alienated from their father to the present day.

"Well—" she cleared her throat "—after my parents divorced, I lived with my mother and my baby sister in Mystery and finished high school there. I know it as well as a native, but with the additional experience of having grown up in many diverse cultures."

"So you feel you would be qualified to handle my affairs in Mystery?"

She might have laughed if she hadn't felt so much like crying. Darkly she wondered how many affairs he was planning to have—hopefully not as many as her father had had.

"Certainly, as your personal assistant, I believe I can handle anything the estate might require. I took accounting in college. I can run a household. Additionally, my experience overseas will help with the management of parties and soirees you might have at the lodge.'' She added, ''I can also help with your wife's schedule.''

''I haven't got a wife.''

Kirsten released an inner sigh of relief. The man's marital status was none of her business, but she was applying for the position of personal assistant, and she certainly didn't look forward to doing anything too personal—such as covering up anything sordid with an unknowing wife waiting in the wings.

''All right, Ms. Meadows, you can go now.''

She opened her mouth as if to ask whether she had gotten the job, but the words didn't come. Somehow they seemed irrelevant. This handsome wealthy man was used to saying who lived and who died in the Wall Street world; her situation with him wouldn't change by asking furtive little questions.

Nodding, she turned to leave.

''The lodge is finished, and I'd like to take a long weekend there to settle in. I'll leave for Montana this evening and show you what I want done there.''

Her back stiffened. It sure sounded as if she had the job.

"The pay issue...?" She broached the subject, turning to face him.

He cut her off. "It's settled. I'll meet your requirements."

"Th-thank you," she stammered, wondering how she'd gone from the despair of failure to total success within seconds.

But he'd already dismissed her. He didn't look up from his desk, or the memo he was reading.

She exited the stifling office, her heart singing.

"Thank you, Hazel, thank you!" she said to herself all the way down the elevator.

Hazel McCallum was the reason she'd even gotten the job. The aging cattle baroness owned almost all of Mystery, Montana. From her ranch she oversaw Mystery Valley as if it was her own personal kingdom, which it almost was. And the seventy-plus-year-old woman thought of every Mystery native as her own kin. It was Hazel who had taken it upon herself to find Kirsten the position as personal assistant to Mystery's newest resident, Seth Morgan.

And Kirsten needed the job. White-collar jobs were hard to come by in cattle country. Her mother and little sister counted on Kirsten both emotionally and financially, and right now nei-

ther one was fit to move elsewhere, to some
other town where they had no support.

Nothing could repay all that Hazel had done
for them. Kirsten would need a lifetime to thank
the woman for all her kindnesses, especially to
Kirsten's mother, who'd been battling illness
and had needed so much more than either Kirsten or her eleven-year-old sister could provide.

Thinking about her mother, Kirsten walked
out of the building and went toward the subway,
eager to get to her hotel room and pack for her
trip back home.

But even as she descended the subway esca-
lator, she was still thanking Hazel under her
breath.

Seth Morgan watched the young woman in
her inexpensive black suit depart his office.

Kirsten Meadows had been more than he'd
expected. Certainly, as Hazel had said, she was
qualified for the job. Unbelievably qualified if
her résumé was any indication. He had no doubt
she would take her work seriously and be an
asset to him.

What he hadn't seen coming was the feeling
he'd had when he'd met her dark blue eyes. Certainly he was attracted to the woman. He was

male, after all, and Kirsten Meadows's face was positively angelic in its beauty.

Yet it was the eyes that had struck him. Eyes dark and deep, like a drowning pool. His defenses had gone up immediately.

He scowled and jammed the button for his secretary.

"Yes, Mr. Morgan?" came the studied melodious voice through the intercom.

"Get me Hazel McCallum on the phone."

"Right away, sir."

He swiveled his chair to face the breathless skyscape of lower Manhattan, of the Statue of Liberty and Governor's Island. The view was magnificent. One could feel as if they'd conquered the world with a panorama like his.

But lately the view had been less satisfying to him. It was certainly a monument to man's achievement. Each building, its architecture and function proclaimed a new conquest.

Yet he wondered if he was getting tired of conquest. There were times when he would stare out at the buildings and wonder if the people inside—the sum of its parts—weren't greater than the whole, not by virtue of conquest, but by virtue of relationships.

Yes, he was growling for something more. But he never quite knew what it was.

Until it was hinted at in a woman's dark blue eyes.

He was pensive for a moment, his own cool gaze darkening with thought. But then his expression hardened and his eyes flashed.

He wasn't going to be tricked, however, and he knew Hazel McCallum well enough to have had wind of her matchmaking schemes to repopulate the town of Mystery with people other than tourists. Her recommendation of Kirsten Meadows had looked fine on paper, but Hazel had known good and well what she looked like, and to dangle her in front of him, well, it was—it was—wicked enough for him to do.

He pushed the button to the buzzing intercom.

"Sir?" came his secretary's hesitant voice. "Ms. McCallum told me she isn't taking phone calls from New York at this time."

"What?" he gasped. Never had someone refused to take his phone call.

"She—she said that if you need to speak with her, you'll have to do as all the residents do in Mystery. You can call at her ranch."

Seth's mouth hardened. His eyes narrowed.

"She did, did she?" He spoke loud and clear into the intercom. "Well, call that old gal up and tell her I want to see her first thing tomorrow morning."

"There or here, sir?"

He could tell even his secretary was intimidated by wily old Hazel McCallum.

"There," he spat, exasperated, feeling like a Victorian suitor who'd finally been permitted to call on the boss's daughter. "And get my plane ready for Montana."

He snapped off the intercom and faced the view again, this time taking solace in the fact that while it wasn't cattle baronesses and blue Montana peaks, he'd conquered something in his life.

Something, at least.

The plane's interior was palomino-blond. The shades and hues of it melted together smoothly, as smooth as the buttery-leather chair Kirsten had sat in for takeoff. They were now at twenty thousand feet and climbing. They flew into the setting sun, the subtle cabin lights turning the interior into a rare, shadowy gold.

The clinking of glass and ice made her look over her shoulder. In the corner of the cabin was a wet bar where a short, natty steward was already preparing drinks. Beyond was another cabin, which held the lavatory and—she still could hardly believe it—a bed where Seth Morgan could nap while he jetted to London or Tokyo.

"—the first week. Then if I happen to be at the ranch I'd like to know that you can handle the correspondence with Mary back in New York." Seth Morgan drilled instructions at her like a marine. "Additionally, I'd like you to work closely with Hazel McCallum in finding me the right kind of trail horses. I will have guests and I want good horses for them in the stable."

"I've ridden since I was six years old—Hazel and I work very well together," Kirsten promised, taking notes on the new laptop Seth had provided.

"What can I get you to drink?" the attendant broke in.

"Water," Seth answered, clearly used to being served.

"Iced tea, please," Kirsten answered, again wondering about the man sitting across from her at the table.

She mused that the sparkling water the attendant poured for him might mean he was a health freak. That would go down hard in Mystery, where steak was considered one of the four food groups.

"Here you go," the attendant purred, holding out a tall iced tea.

She took it.

"Sugar?" the attendant offered, lowering the silver tray so she could reach the sterling sugar bowl.

A violent burst of turbulence hit the plane at precisely the moment she reached for the sugar spoon.

Kirsten watched Seth Morgan toss his sparkling water down the front of his perfect Italian suit. She might even have laughed had she not been doused by the iced tea in her hand, then sugared like a warm cookie with the contents of the sugar bowl.

"Oh, dear Lord!" the attendant squealed, horrified at the mess.

"I'm sorry," Kirsten murmured, instinctively licking her sugary lips, desperate to wipe down the expensive leather seat before even thinking of herself.

Seth Morgan sat frozen across from her, staring, a hard expression on his face.

She was convinced he was furious.

"I'll pay to have the leather cleaned," she added, looking for more napkins for the mess.

"Nonsense," he said, standing.

She was trapped, her front so full of sugar she looked as if she'd just been snowed upon.

Slowly he leaned over to her, easing off her black jacket. His hands were surprisingly warm when they brushed her nape.

For some reason she'd expected cold hands from him. He was rich, handsome, powerful. She'd expected cold hands to go along with a cold heart.

"Well, this won't do." The steward tsked.

She looked down. The white T-shirt she'd worn beneath her jacket was transparent with tea. Gasping, she covered herself with her arms, the sticky sugar only spreading. She prayed Seth Morgan hadn't been thinking what the steward had, but when she looked up and met his eyes, she could see very well that he'd viewed everything right down to the color of her pink bra.

"You'll need to change," he said woodenly, his gaze still dark and penetrating, as if he, too, were thinking of sex.

"M-my bag's in the hold below. I didn't think I'd need it," she stammered, shivering.

"You can't fly to Montana like that. We still have hours to go."

"Maybe I can clean up in the lavatory."

He nodded to the steward. "Give Miss Meadows my bathrobe and whatever she needs to shower. When we land, we'll deliver her bag in here and she can change.''

The steward nodded.

Kirsten gingerly rose from the chair, holding her wet front and trying to contain all the sugar. She followed the steward into the rear cabin, her mind captured by Seth Morgan's stare, dark and full of wicked promise.

All she could think of during her shower was that she and her new boss were off to a turbulent start—no pun intended—and she only feared it would get worse. If there was one thing she already knew about her boss, it was that he was a predator. She would need all her faculties to survive around him. After her father's treatment of her mother, the only plan she could count on was never to be the man's prey. That was looking difficult now that she'd been sugared like a warm cookie and served up for his pleasure.

The shampoo bottle slipped from her wet fingers, the clatter jangling her already frayed nerves. But she comforted herself with the thought that he could rattle her all he wanted; as long as he paid her well, and as long as she stayed emotionally invulnerable he could have all the cookies he wanted.

Two

Now, how in the hell, Seth wondered as he sipped his second whiskey, was he going to get that image out of his mind?

The picture of Kirsten Meadows, wet and sticky, crystals of sugar clinging to her eyelashes like a dusting of snow, well, it was one damn vision no man would ever forget. She'd looked up at him like a lush, sexual, crystalline fairy, and if he'd been infinitesimally less civilized, he'd have made love to her right there in her seat.

He shifted uncomfortably and stared into the blackness outside the plane window.

The steward had taken a seat up front with the pilots. Alone, Seth could still hear running water from the lavatory over the drone of the jet engines.

The woman had thick blond hair, and it was going to take a long, hot shower to get all the sugar out of it. Against his will he thought of his own hands running through her wet hair, scrubbing the sweetness out of it.

He shifted again, and took another deep swig of the whiskey. The side of his hand was sticky where he'd helped her out of her jacket. Without thinking, he licked it. He closed his eyes, savoring the task. Plain table sugar had been made into nectar just by the addition of desire.

He wasn't just randy, that was for sure. Nikki, his model girlfriend du jour, was happy to comply with his needs, especially since he'd bought her a red sports car and ruby earrings to match it.

But something unfamiliar was happening to him. Instead of wishing Nikki could fly to Montana that night for an intimate encounter, he dreaded the planned upcoming weekend he'd promised her. He no longer wanted to show Nikki the new ranch. Now he just wanted to prowl around it on his own so he could size up his new employee.

"May I come in?"

His head snapped around, and he saw Kirsten standing in the cabin door, her small curvy form wrapped in a paisley robe the exact midnight blue of her eyes.

"Take a seat. We've got at least two more hours of flying time."

She cautiously walked barefoot through the cabin, clutching the cashmere lapels of the robe together at her neckline like a spinster. Her innocent gesture charmed him in a way, but not enough for him to stop staring at her like a wolf-hound.

Meeting his gaze, she twisted her rose-colored mouth into a rueful grin and said, "I have to say that's never happened to me before—but then, I've only taken commercial flights and they put their sugar in those little packets. I now know why." She laughed nervously.

He laughed, too. It felt good. It released the tension in the cabin and the terrible tension in his body.

"I'll have to tell Ricky to get some of those," he offered.

She laughed again. Her face lit up. "Is that his name? The steward? We hardly got to know each other."

"Yes, well, he got to know you," Seth said,

his words more caustic than he'd meant them to be.

A silence permeated the cabin.

Slowly she rose and went to get her laptop. Flustered, she said, "I guess we can finish now—"

"I'm no longer working." He raised his nearly empty whiskey glass and gestured to the bar. "Help yourself. It might do you good. You seem to be still shivering."

She glanced over at the bar, unsure.

"Go ahead. I won't hold it against you tomorrow. God knows I needed a drink." With that, he emptied his glass and returned to staring out the window.

Warily she stepped to the bar and fixed herself a drink. He was a strange man, but perhaps great wealth did that to a person. And yet there was something about him that transcended the money. Something primeval, earthy. Visceral. She saw it in his stare and in the way he always seemed to be shifting in his seat. Shifting because he couldn't quite seem to get comfortable.

She doubled her drink and wondered if the restlessness was catching. She certainly was restless every time she met that dark, disapproving stare.

*   *   *

By her second drink, Kirsten was getting over her unease. The silence grew into an exchange of pleasantries, finally to actual talk. Seth asked a lot of personal questions—no, rather demanded answers to a lot of personal questions, but Kirsten didn't mind answering him. She just explained away, the hum of the jet engines strongly comforting.

"There isn't a whole lot more to be said. After that, my mom and my sister moved back to Mystery. And here we are today. Just hunky-dory." Kirsten sat cross-legged in her seat, her hand nursing the best whiskey and soda she'd ever tasted. The liquor left her sleepy and mellow. Even as harsh as Seth Morgan could look, she didn't mind it so much now. Now that the ice had broken, and they were talking.

"Why were you so hungry for this job?" His pointed question sent a chill down her spine.

"Hey, I could have worked flipping burgers at the Mystery Diner, but do you know what they pay?" She averted her gaze with a laugh.

"Hazel said you had to have this job. You needed the money."

Depression crept into her like the whiskey. "Carrie's only eleven, and my mom—well—she's been having some health problems lately. She really can't work."

"So everything's fallen on you."

Kirsten fell silent. Finally she said, "I didn't need Hazel to help me find a job, but I confess, if this can work out, I'd really like that."

Desperate to change the subject, she gave the cabin a cursory glance. "I can't believe I just took a shower on an airplane. I mean, how do you get used to all this?"

It was his turn to fall silent. He stared at her for a long curious moment.

Eventually he said, "I used to be hungry for things, too. I wanted the world in my lap, and then I got it. I guess I'm jaded about riches now. It takes a lot to make me want something these days."

"It must be great to have all your appetites appeased," she said quietly. "I just get hungrier and hungrier."

"My appetites are far from sated. And I always get what I want."

His words seemed more like a threat than a statement.

She studied him, a warning tingle creeping down her spine.

He said no more after that.

He only stared into the darkness out the window, dismissing her as if she had grown invisible.

*   *   *

The plane landed on time. When the steward Ricky brought Kirsten her luggage, she changed into a pair of jeans and a thermal shirt. Seth had a Jeep waiting for him at the airport and in no time they took off for the new ranch.

It was not what she'd expected.

After seeing his office, she figured Seth Morgan's ranch house would be a sprawling mansion tacked onto the side of a mountain. Instead, what she found was a master-crafted log house settled snugly into the land like a bird in a nest. The house was immensely livable. Fieldstone fireplaces graced each room. The ranch house didn't even have an office. Seth explained that he'd bought a ranch in Montana to relax, not work.

Against her better judgment to remain aloof, Kirsten was impressed by the building and the man.

The housekeeper, Viola, was an older woman with close-cropped white hair and high cheekbones that hinted at Native ancestry. She showed Kirsten her room and kindly left her with a tea tray.

Kirsten looked around the beautiful bedroom done warmly in aqua-blue cashmere, then threw herself on the bed and went right to the phone to call her family.

"Carrie! Tell Mom I'm back and I got the job!" Kirsten whispered excitedly into the phone.

She waited until she heard the familiar voice and then continued, "That's right. I got the job! So tomorrow you quit at the diner. No more work. You need to get over the chemo and be happy again. That way you'll be as healthy as the doctor says you are."

Her mom's expected protests fell on deaf ears.

"I've got it covered, Mom," Kirsten insisted. "You should see the room I have over here. Just the fabric of the bedcover is like my best pash-mina shawl, so what do I need the rent money for? It's yours. You must quit tomorrow. I'm going by to thank Hazel in the morning, and I'll stop by then to check on you guys."

She listened for a minute and rolled her eyes. "It's done. Accept it. Everything has worked out just the way I planned. Our ship has come in. Kiss Carrie for me."

She hung up the phone, then hugged herself. It had been the best of days. All her problems seemed to be over.

But then she heard the knock and looked up. Standing in her still-open doorway was Seth

Morgan. He wore only jeans and a wool plaid shirt. He'd even kicked back so much that he was barefoot, but by the look of displeasure on his face he certainly couldn't be described as relaxed.

"Your ship would like a word with you about tomorrow," he said.

She rose cat-style from the bed. Her face heated with embarrassment. "I'm sorry you heard that—"

"Miss Meadows, no one knows my net worth better than I do," he said cuttingly. "If you hadn't noticed, I would have thought you stupid."

He gave her a dismissive look. "Now, on to business. I would like to take what Jim, the ranch manager, has in the barn right now and see which horses will fit my houseguests when I have them. I'd like a second opinion on the horseflesh, so tomorrow you can expect a fair amount of time in the saddle."

"Certainly," she choked out, near tears that her precious job might be threatened by another stupid mistake.

"I'll see you first thing in the morning."

"I'll be ready," she said in a raspy voice. "In the meantime, do you need me to do anything for you tonight?"

His long, hungry stare might have shocked her if she hadn't already been so afraid. His cold gaze raked her lips, then dragged down her throat, finally lingering on her thermal shirt and the way it stretched over her full chest.

"I'll see you in the morning, Miss Meadows." He abruptly turned and left.

She walked to the door and shut it. Alone in her room, she breathed deeply, trying to release the adrenaline pumping through her body.

She couldn't afford to offend the man. She would have to be scrupulously careful in the future. Too much depended on her.

But when her initial fears ebbed, her heart still raced with a strange excitement. She closed her eyes and could still see him in her doorway, his face hard and handsome, his jeans shrugged on over bare feet as if he was just anyone, rather than a billionaire.

The signals her body gave her put her into raging denial. Her breasts, her lips tingled just from his stare. She dreaded to think how she would react should he ever try to touch her. Her conflict certainly had something to do with the fact that Seth Morgan was a man, and an extremely attractive man at that. The gulf between them economically was too large to bridge, and more than that, she didn't want to get hurt, not the way her mother had been hurt by her father.

As her father had gained stature as an expatriate, he'd decided to trade up on his wives. Kirsten believed he was on his fourth right now, and this one was younger than she was.

Certainly, if her father who had only some power could do what he had to her mother, then Seth Morgan would be able to put her in a blender.

So he was not worth it and never would be.

Exhausted, she slipped out of her clothes and found her nightgown in her luggage. Sliding beneath the sheets, she was determined to put Seth out of her mind. She would do the job perfectly, and anything else that might be messy she would stay away from. She would keep theirs a straightforward relationship. A piece of cake. All she had to do was be professional and everything would be fine.

But as tired as she was, she still couldn't get the picture of him out of her mind.

And despite how well everything had been laid out in her mind, she hardly slept at all that night.

Kirsten and Seth had been out on the trail for more than an hour. ''Over there is Blue Rock

Creek where I used to go swimming in the summer." Kirsten pointed to the west of the trail.

She sat atop a plump dappled mare named Sterling, and Seth rode a tall dark stallion more Thoroughbred than quarter horse, named Noir. Both animals were the best-trained horses Kirsten had ever seen, and so it was a pleasure to venture forth on the trail until they were beyond the tree line and well into high country.

"Did you take your horse up here then? Back when you were younger?" he asked.

Shaking her head, she said, "I never had my own horse. We could never afford it, but sure, I trailed here. Hazel was always willing to lend a good rider a horse. Whenever I had a down moment as a teen, all I had to do was ask and she'd give me one of her best barrel racers. And after a long ride up here to heaven, nothing seemed so bad anymore. Nothing."

She glanced at him and smiled. Still nervous from the encounter the night before, she'd been reluctant to open up, but once on the familiar trail with a good horse beneath her, she was in her element again and she felt in control once more.

"I even saw a grizzly up here once," she confessed. "She scared me half to death. And you know, it was a worst case scenario. The grizzly even had two cubs with her.''

"You were lucky she didn't come at you," he said, turning a concerned eye to her.

Shrugging, she dismissed the danger. "She was on the other side of the creek, and I'm sure she wanted as little to do with me as I did with her. In fact, I can still remember what I thought back then. I thought of my own mother, who was protecting her cubs by bringing them back to Mystery." She released a dark ironic smile. "It's funny. I guess I'm the mother with the cubs now."

He seemed to freeze in the saddle. Slowly he queried, "How many children do you have?"

She wasn't sure if she'd heard him right. "Did you ask how many children I have?"

"Yes," came the wooden reply.

"Does that factor into the job description?" she asked, unsure where he was going with the questions.

"If you have children, I will understand that you may not want to stay at the ranch. I can give you a bungalow instead—"

Laughing, she shook her head. "Thanks for the offer, but the only child I have is an eleven-year-old sister named Carrie."

And a mother who's weak from a successful dose of chemo, she added to herself.

"I like children." His expression was scrupulously washed of all emotion.

"Did you come from a large family, then?" The question, she thought, was perfectly appropriate and not out of line.

He surprised her when he laughed. "I was the only child, raised—if you could call it that—entirely by my mother."

"My parents divorced, too," she mentioned, gaze trailing to the jagged purple horizon iced with snow.

"My parents weren't divorced. That would have been too honest." Giving her a penetrating stare, he added, "My father was a successful financier. He was absent from our lives, always away, having too much fun without us."

"I'm sorry," she offered, her hand stroking Sterling's salt-and-pepper mane as if to comfort. "But at least your mother was there for you."

He gave her an amused, jaded look. "You know that old joke about the couple going into the restaurant—the husband sees another woman there and gives her a big French kiss?"

She shook her head.

He continued. "Well, when the couple sit down, the wife asks him who the woman is and he tells her it's his mistress. The wife is furious and she wants a divorce, but then the husband explains that if she divorces him, gone is the winter cabin in Aspen and the house in St. Thomas, no more shopping sprees in Boca, and so on.''

Smirking, he turned Noir around to face her. "So the joke ends that the wife shuts up about getting a divorce, and then when they see a couple next to them in the restaurant and the man is kissing a woman they know is not his wife, the woman asks who the woman is, and the husband says it's the man's mistress.''

A long pause ensued for effect.

At last he gave the punch line. Slowly he said, "So then the wife comments, 'Well, *our* mistress is prettier.' ''

Kirsten rode silently on, not sure if she wanted to laugh or cry. The joke was awful, but it certainly told of a woman more interested in her shopping sprees in Boca than her son.

"So you see," he said, turning Noir around and continuing the rocky trail heavenward, "sometimes divorce is much more honest."

They rode for a long time, each in their own thoughts.

Wanting to break the silence, she finally said,

"Hey, do you want to see where I saw the grizzly by Blue Rock Creek?"

He turned and nodded.

They took the fork in the trail that led to the creek.

Once there, she dismounted and haltered Sterling. Seth did the same.

"I think it's downstream from here. Do you still want to see? It might be a bit of a hike." She looked up at him.

Without her heels on, she suddenly realized how tall he was. He towered over her. Intimidated enough by his brooding dark looks and penetrating stare, she had no need for a reminder that he was physically much stronger than she was.

"No problem for me, but it's rocky—that okay with you?"

She laughed. "Hey, this is my childhood haunt. I could do it blindfolded."

"Then show me."

She took a second look at him to be sure it was what he wanted, then she wandered along the creek edge until weeds choked her path and she was forced to walk in the creek.

He followed, his cowboy boots sloshing along behind her.

"It's not far, I don't think." She chewed on

her lower lip. "It's been a while, though." She walked another few steps. Beyond was the clearing of soapberries that had once hidden the mother grizzly bear and her two cubs.

"There it is. I was standing over there—" She turned to the other bank and her leather-soled cowboy boot slid on a mossy stone. She went flying.

A steely arm went around her waist, catching her.

She looked up, wanting only to give Seth a gratifying glance before stepping out of his arms, but he wouldn't let go. She stood there staring up at him. There was nothing around them but silence. Even the crickets, it seemed, were holding their breath.

"Is our mistress going to be prettier?" he asked, looking down at her, cynicism like a poison in his voice.

She locked gazes with him, devastated yet strangely thrilled at the same time. His arm was like a prison, and his eyes pinned her to the ground. His words stung and promised at the same time. He implied marriage and commitment, all the while assuring her of deception and heartache.

Her pulse beat a staccato in her throat, her lips grew dry and she licked them—just as she had done when doused with table sugar. The water rushing at their feet now became deafening.

"There won't be any mistresses in my marriage. I promise you." Her voice was thick with emotion.

He arched one jet-black eyebrow. "What's to stop them?" His own words grew husky. "This?" he whispered right before he crushed her to him and captured her lips with his.

The kiss was molten lava. Almost more than she could bear. It had been months since she'd been kissed by a man with so much yearning, months since she'd allowed herself the sexual pleasure of one deep earthy kiss.

She opened her mouth to him, selfishly taking what he had to offer. He didn't disappoint. His scent filled her. Whereas she'd thought he'd smell of Bond Street cologne and plastic, instead her nostrils filled with man heat and leather. It was delicious.

He pulled her farther into the hard wall of his body, his kiss deepening with his tongue. She released a nearly silent moan, her hands curling against his chest as he penetrated her mouth with lover's strokes. Her legs weakened; her head grew light. Only her yearning remained sharp and hungry, driving her mindlessly toward ultimate satisfaction.

His palm rubbed the inward curve of her waist, then made its way up her torso. She didn't want sanity to intervene, but she knew if he cupped her breast she would be well on her way to sleeping with her boss. And that was unforgivable madness.

Cold logic forced her return to earth.

As if drugged, she pulled back from him, and with a kitten's fury she spat out, "Look, I've heard about you. I know all about your conquests, all the beautiful girls. Hazel told me you're the talk of Wall Street." Her passion rose. "But I don't want to be another conquest, okay? I don't need the trouble. What I want— what I need is this job. I must have this job, and I won't be able to keep it if you and I—well— if you and I—"

Her frustration, sexual and otherwise, choked her. "Well, we won't do it, okay? We just will not!" she cried before she ran down the creek to her horse and galloped all the way back to the stable.

"Hazel, you're setting me up," Seth growled that evening in Hazel McCallum's nineteenth-century parlor. Ebby, Hazel's housekeeper, seemed to sense where the conversation was going and brought over the whiskey decanter.

"You calling me a sneaky varmint? Seth, you told me you needed a personal assistant, and I recommended one. Now look at you! Sitting there accusing me of rustlin'," she said.

Hazel, with her blue jeans and cowboy boots that were the perfect foil for her silver hair with its elegant chignon, nodded to Ebby to pour two stiff whiskeys.

Seth waved his away.

Hazel took hers, unable to hide the twinkle in her famous Prussian-blue eyes. She commented, "I always like a snort before dinner. Gets my blood up, don't you think? Oh, but yours is already up, I guess...." She lifted the glass to her lips.

He resentfully took his whiskey.

"I really don't think Miss Meadows is the type of woman I was looking for to fill the position," he said in clipped tones.

"Why?" Hazel retorted good-naturedly. "Because she's beautiful and smart? She's fluent in five languages, too. I believe you're only fluent in one, if my sources are correct."

Giving her his notorious icy stare, he said, "Yes, but I'm fluent in the only language that counts—money. So that makes me fluent in every language."

"Kirsten Meadows doesn't speak that language. Just you remember that, Seth.'' Hazel turned serious.

His mouth turned into a hard line. ''I've never met a woman who didn't speak it. Besides, that's not what our dear Miss Meadows was saying on the phone about her ship coming in.''

The aging cattle baroness studied him. ''She's not like those other women. You mark my words—she's something you've never dealt with before, son, and God save you if you forget that.''

He said nothing. The line of his mouth grew harder.

Hazel laughed and refilled his glass.

''Now, on to more pleasant talk,'' she continued. ''I meant to tell you that you're hosting next week's Mystery BBQ Sizzle. We have it once a year in the summer, and I usually host it here at the ranch, but it's time the townsfolk got to know the carpetbagger in their midst.''

''Don't tell me, tell Kirsten. I may have to be in New York—''

''I don't give a damn where you might have to be. When I sold you that prized parcel of my land, I told you it came with a commitment to the town—and that means being here.'' She winked. ''Why don't you invite your fancy New

York friends? They might get a kick out of seeing you play ranch hand.''

He finally laughed. ''Hazel, you're in the
wrong element here in this little town of Mystery. I swear you're diabolical enough to work
on Wall Street.''

The cattle baroness smiled at his flash of
white, even teeth. ''Why, this ol' cowgirl
couldn't handle them city slickers, and you
know it.''

''No, they couldn't handle you,'' he said
wryly.

''We'll give them the chance to find out a
week from Friday.''

He took another long sip of whiskey. And
rolled his eyes.

''Hazel! I just had to get here and tell you! I
got the—'' Kirsten screeched to a halt in the
parlor, Ebby at her heels.

''Oh, gosh, I'm sorry, Hazel. You have company,'' she muttered, her gaze going to Seth.

''Nonsense. He's family now just like you are,
Kirsten. He bought that land of mine and that
makes him a native son.''

Hazel got to her feet—she was slower than
she used to be, but more spritely than most her
age. ''Now that you're here, we're just about to

have some vittles. Come take a place at the table.''

Ebby disappeared to add the third place setting.

Kirsten still shook her head apologetically. ''No, forgive me. I should have called....''

''Since when do I answer my phone?'' Hazel harrumphed. ''If you got words to say to me, you say 'em to my face just like in the good ol' days, or you keep 'em to yourself. So now you two pokes come to dinner before your plate gets cold.'' Hazel left the parlor for the dining room.

Kirsten was alone with Seth.

She looked up at her boss, her emotions still stinging from their encounter in the creek just hours before.

Awkwardly she said, ''How do you do, Mr. Morgan.''

''Miss Meadows,'' he acknowledged curtly.

She swore there was a twinkle in his cold eyes. Her cheeks heated.

''I hope you don't mind my barging in like this. I truly didn't realize you were here.''

He gave a wry twist to his lips, the lips she still found wickedly evocative and handsome. ''Not at all. But if we're going to work together, and now dine together, I'd like you to call me Seth.''

"Certainly. And you may call me Kirsten."

He nodded.

Even she could see how stiff they were with each other. The kiss that afternoon had seemed to freeze both of them.

"Drink?" Ebby interrupted, offering Kirsten a whiskey and ice.

Grateful to have something to focus on other than the memory of their kiss, she took the proffered glass and sipped it.

"She's waiting," Ebby announced, a knowing smile on her lips.

Seth rolled his eyes again. "Oh, I know, one thing we don't do is keep the queen waiting."

Both Ebby and Kirsten stared at him.

Then they both burst out laughing.

Ebby finally interjected with, "You know, Mr. Morgan, you're a quick study, and you seem to be getting things a lot faster than most. I think you might fit here in Mystery after all."

Three

———

Hazel's dinners were famous for their overindulgence, and the current night was no exception. Kirsten was half-tipsy and full to the gills when she and Seth said good-night to the cattle baroness. Having gotten a ride to Hazel's ranch from her mother, Kirsten reluctantly accepted Seth's offer for a ride back to his place.

The mountainous road was no match for her emotions as she sat next to Seth in his Jeep. Playing elk slalom, he navigated the vehicle with skill and precision through the dark rural night.

"You drive like a native," she commented.

He chuckled. "I'm no native. I grew up in East Hampton in New York."

"Well, something's clicking with you and Mystery. The tourists are terrified of the roads at night."

"My parents had a ski lodge in Big Sky, Montana. I decided early on that I like the nature of the mountains more than the skiing. Camping made me learn to drive the winding roads."

"That explains it."

He looked sideways at her, studying her.

"You know," he interjected into the quiet automobile, "Hazel told me that next week I have to host the Mystery BBQ Sizzle. I hope you know what has to be done, because I don't have a clue how to go about something like that."

It was her turn to chuckle. "Hazel's so tricky. She loves handing that over to the greenhorns. It's like a test."

"Well, I expect you as my personal assistant to make sure I pass the test."

She nodded. "I know what has to be done. No problem. Consider it a finished deal."

"I'll want to invite some New Yorkers."

"Certainly."

"I'll leave the list for you in the morning. You can find all their numbers in my files."

"Of course."

"I'll want the plane sent for Nikki."

Her heart went thump. She knew who Nikki Butler was. The tabloids loved to photograph the willowy model with her billionaire boyfriends.

Kirsten denied any pangs of jealousy.

The kiss she and Seth had experienced that afternoon was at best an inconvenience, at worst a threat to the job she dearly needed. The emotions that roiled inside her upon hearing this could only be disappointment—disappointment to find out her boss was so shallow as to date an airhead model with an IQ less than her daily calorie intake.

"I'll make sure she has everything she wants."

Including you, Kirsten thought with more bitterness than even she had expected.

"See that she comes in on Thursday so we have some time alone before the big event."

Woodenly Kirsten responded, "I'll take care of it."

"If you have any questions as to her preferences, Mary can help you with them. She knows everything about Ms. Butler."

She nodded, wondering if her face looked as green in the dashboard light as she felt.

"Do you feel all right, Kirsten?"

Her head snapped around to face him. "I feel great. Why wouldn't I? Why would you ask?"

He paused. "Well, we've been parked at the ranch for almost a minute now. You seem preoccupied."

Kirsten felt as if she was waking from a nightmare.

Suddenly she looked out of the Jeep window and realized they had indeed stopped at the front of Seth's house. She couldn't remember coming to a halt at all.

"No, no. I'm fine. Just a little tired from the long day," she blathered, getting out of the jeep.

"Well, good night, then."

Like an idiot, she kept on blathering. "I'll take care of everything. Don't worry. In two days every preparation will be made."

"Good night, Miss Meadows."

She paused, suddenly hating the formality when before there had been none.

"Good night, Mr. Morgan."

The Mystery BBQ Sizzle was the event of the summer. Tourists and locals alike attended. It was a tradition of Hazel McCallum's that went back decades. Hazel always said you could find out more about a person at a barbecue than you could at a five-star hotel.

Kirsten, watching supermodel Nikki Butler sunning her long svelte self at the ranch's pool, had the sickening feeling Hazel was right. She was going to get a load of Nikki Butler's character that weekend whether she wanted to or not.

"Could you stock the pool fridge with more mineral water?" Nikki asked Viola the housekeeper in a sweet voice.

Viola smiled as she walked past Kirsten.

"Can I get you anything?" the older woman asked, as always, eternally gracious.

"Don't add me to your woes. I'm strictly self-serve around here," Kirsten offered with a smile of her own.

"It's only going to get worse when the rest of the guests arrive. He's got another model and two brokers coming tomorrow," Viola added.

Kirsten almost shuddered. "There'll be a run on Scotch and rice cakes in town."

Laughing, Viola went toward the kitchen.

Kirsten was about to leave also when she saw Seth enter the pool area from the stables. He didn't see her; he seemed to have eyes only for Nikki.

Stepping behind a rough-hewn pillar, Kirsten watched, a sickening feeling in her stomach. She didn't want to get involved with Seth Morgan, but she feared her rational mind was telling her one thing, and her heart and hormones another.

Seeing him interact with another woman was not something she enjoyed, but she couldn't look away. Her curiosity took over.

They were discussing something. Neither seemed particularly demonstrative toward each other, but Kirsten wondered if she herself was putting a spin on that.

Seth seemed to settle an issue, and Nikki, appearing as self-involved as Kirsten expected, simply sat back in her lounge chair and resumed tanning.

Not wanting him to see her, Kirsten darted behind the cabana and walked toward the house. She went to the desk in the large kitchen and absentmindedly went through her list for the barbecue.

"Miss Meadows—"

Kirsten was startled. Seth stood right behind her, studying her with that wintergreen gaze.

"Yes?" she answered coolly.

"Nikki needs to call her agent—would you bring her her cell phone? She said it's on the bed."

She nodded.

He almost seemed to want to smirk. But he added nothing else before he walked away.

Fuming, Kirsten went up the rough-hewn staircase.

Besides her room and Seth's suite, there were three guest rooms at the back of the house. Hoping and praying she wouldn't have to go looking for the cell phone on Seth's bed, she went to the back of the hall.

All three guest bedrooms were unoccupied.

Nikki must be staying with Seth, Kirsten thought.

Strangely disheartened, she went toward Seth's closed door.

They'd shared only a kiss and a few pleasant moments. There was nothing between them, and his girlfriend had every right to stay wherever she wanted while in his home.

Nikki Butler was his girlfriend. His *girlfriend,* she repeated to herself silently.

She was going to have to remember that while Nikki was here—and most especially once the model left. Seth Morgan was dangerous. He played the field and cared nothing of the women he left in his wake.

After what had happened to her mother, Kirsten was doubly appalled that she'd had even a fleeting thought of a relationship with the handsome lout. Her own experience with men had been wary, at best. She'd made her own bad choices. One in particular, James, was even still hanging around Mystery, nagging her for more dates even though they'd broken it off after James had lost his temper one night. She had no patience for that kind of man, and so far she'd met few that weren't like her father—narcissistic.

So she and her new boss had had one kiss, Kirsten told herself. It meant nothing. It was an error in judgment by both of them, and that was all. The fire in her mouth when he'd deepened the kiss was all that seemed to affect her brain lately, but what she'd have to concentrate on was how cold her feet had been with the stream rushing around her boots. The coldness was what she needed to concentrate on now. Just the coldness.

She opened the waxed knotty-pine door to his bedroom.

Her expression froze.

The perfect specimen of a naked man's backside stood between her and the bed.

"Oh, I'm sorry!" she gasped, the blood draining from her face.

"What the hell are you doing here?" Seth snapped, holding his swim trunks—which obviously he hadn't had time to put on yet—in front of himself when he turned to face her.

Speechless, all she could do was stare at him,

her gaze taking in the grid of muscle on his belly and the dark trail of hair that pointed like an arrow to...to...

"Again, what the hell are you doing here? Don't you knock?" he asked, his voice laced with anger.

"I'm sorry, but you told me to get Ms. Butler's phone on the bed. I didn't think you were in here."

A muscle bunched in his jaw. "She's staying in the cabin. Along with everyone else from New York."

"I'm—I'm sorry," she stammered. "I just assumed she was staying up here."

"She's not."

Why not? she wanted to cry out, desperate to make sense of this man so she could protect herself.

But there was no asking questions now. He had no clothes on, and his relationship with Nikki was none of her business. None absolutely.

Kirsten needed to concentrate on coldness.

And it was very hard to think about the cold as she stared at a naked Seth Morgan, his high, tight buttocks reflecting back at her from a cheval mirror.

"Miss Meadows, you're excused." His gaze

raked her. "Unless, of course, you want to come in and lock the door."

Backing away as if from a bee sting, she shook her head and fumbled for the door. His nudity frightened and aroused her, all at the same time. It brought a rush of emotions she longed to repress. Horrified, she wondered how she would ever keep him from her thoughts when she now had him burned forever in her memory.

She took her escape gladly. She ran from the bedroom, his laughter following her the entire way.

"He's being his usual obnoxious self. I mean, he has the nerve to put me in the guest cabin with everyone else, can you believe it?"

Nikki's upset words to her agent over her cell phone registered all too well with Kirsten when she arrived shortly after retrieving Nikki's cell phone from the guest cabin for her. The model was in a difficult mood in spite of languishing by the pool, and Kirsten could almost sympathize with her. That morning she herself wasn't feeling too gracious, either.

"Oh, honey," Nikki called out to her, her hand on the mouthpiece, "can you see to it that I've got a magnum of champagne in the cabin?

Thanks.'' She went back to her cell phone.
''That ought to do it.''

''Certainly,'' Kirsten said, her insides crawl-
ing at the name *honey*. To Nikki everyone was
honey—Viola, Kirsten, Jim the ranch manager.
The only one who wasn't was Seth Morgan.

Kirsten got the champagne from the wine cellar and brought it to the guest cabin that was
nestled in the rock just out of view from the
house. Setting a couple of crystal flutes on the
copper counter, she placed the champagne in the
fridge, her thoughts a million miles away from
her task.

In many ways Nikki Butler was perfect for
Seth. She was gloriously beautiful, so much so
that their mistress would be hard-pressed to be
prettier. Nikki would also tolerate any of Seth's
bad behavior to get her hands on the next bit of
loot, and all would be happy.

But for some reason the thought of Nikki and
Seth just made Kirsten sad. Certainly Seth Morgan was one of the most cynical, jaded men she
had ever met. But there was something inside
him, something very human. As numb as he was
to intolerable behavior, at least he was cynical
about it. It showed some kind of fight in him,
some kind of reaction to it all instead of being
blithely accepting.

Hazel saw something in him, too, and one day Kirsten wanted to ask her about it. The cattle baroness never ever sold her land. For her to have given Seth an unheard-of amount of family land meant Hazel viewed him as worthwhile.

Kirsten smiled to herself. Ironic though it was, it was hard to see Seth's worth at times, with all the blinding riches around him.

From the window she watched as Seth arrived at the pool. He took a dive off the board, splashing Nikki. His head broke the surface, and he was all wolfish smile and glittering water. Behind him, the mountains ripped upward, their cracked tops frozen with ice.

His wealth could dig a hole in the ground and build a pool, an unnecessary extravagance in the cool Montana summer, but there was nothing the man could do about the mountains. The mountains were there, untouchable and magnificent. The pool and the mountains—style versus substance.

And Kirsten wanted substance, while Nikki wanted style.

Kirsten supposed that was what bothered her. She told herself she wasn't necessarily falling for Seth Morgan. Sure, they'd kissed, and it had been…well, breathtaking. Like the mountains.

But deep down she suspected that Seth Morgan was more than just style.

Yet Nikki would win. It was inevitable.

And then there would be no more hot kisses, no more cold streams rushing through their legs, no more talks on horseback. There would be no more mountains.

Strangely depressed, Kirsten sighed and gathered herself. She wasn't necessarily falling in love with Seth, but at times it sure felt like it.

Like now, when she watched him frolic with his model by the pool. In truth, Kirsten wanted to rip him away from the whole scene, to ease her jealousy.

To ease the heartache she felt whenever she saw things of substance slip away.

Four

Friday afternoon Kirsten watched the men set up the bandstand for the barbecue.

The two-step band she'd hired was one she knew well. She only hoped that James, the lead singer in Mystery's best cowboy band, would let bygones be bygones.

They'd dated for less than a month, and it just hadn't been right. Their personalities didn't mesh, but worse than that, James hadn't understood her. He'd continually mistaken her reserve and caution for being stuck-up.

It wouldn't have worked with James, but he'd

been sore when she'd told him. She only prayed he was attached to someone else by now. Otherwise the barbecue could be most unpleasant, because James had the ability to swill beer like a good ol' boy.

Pushing her anxieties aside, she watched another group of workers set down a portable oak dance floor for two-stepping.

All in all it looked as if the barbecue should be a success. The weather was supposed to be warm and dry. A beautiful Montana sky full of stars was the perfect backdrop for waltzing.

She looked away for a moment, suddenly feeling more like Cinderella than the boss's assistant. The fantasy of dancing in the arms of a man she loved beneath her beloved Montana sky was too much to resist. But every time the daydream took hold, the man she found herself dancing with was Seth Morgan. And that only depressed her more.

"Have the others arrived from the airport yet?" Nikki whined, sipping her umpteenth glass of chardonnay.

Kirsten saw that the model had left poolside just to speak to her.

"I don't know. Their flight was to arrive by now, but I haven't seen Mr. Morgan in the Jeep." Kirsten eyed the tall, beautiful model.

As horrible as it had been to get through last night without thinking of Seth and Nikki together, Kirsten almost believed Nikki was having a harder time. The woman looked caved-in, and she'd been at the wine since way before noon.

Kirsten bit back all the questions she had. Her boss's relationship with his girlfriend was not her concern, but there were so many things going through her head. As it was, hope and despair played a ridiculous game of tug-of-war inside her heart, and she really wanted the torture to end.

"He'd better show up soon," the model sniped, "that's all I know. If he's going to fly me to the middle of nowhere and take away all my fun, then I damn well plan on getting some from Rick."

Shocked, Kirsten at least put together that Rick was one of Seth's friends coming to town from New York.

"Maybe he's just distracted—you know, getting the barbecue together and all." Kirsten wondered why she was even speaking. First of all, it was clear the model didn't want her advice and sympathy any more than she'd want that from a table leg. And if Kirsten were truthful to herself, she knew good and well she didn't want to encourage a relationship between Nikki and Seth. Seth sure as all-fire wasn't getting the barbecue together; rather, that was Kirsten's job, and she had the pulled-out hair to show for it.

"Distracted!" Nikki snorted. "He's the last man to turn down a night of passion. I should know. When I hit the cover of that lingerie catalog, he was all over me."

Kirsten could definitely feel a headache coming on.

"And now," the model rambled, half-drunk, "now he calls me all the way from New York to visit his lodge and puts me in the guest house—the cheating jerk." Nikki looked at her. "So who is the other woman? Has he been inviting someone else up here?"

Kirsten's heart stopped.

Paling, she stammered, "I—I have no idea."

"C'mon. I know you're just protecting the boss, but really, woman to woman, is it that actress he was seen with his last night in New York? Or is he going back to that Parisian as everyone says he will?"

Stupefied, Kirsten didn't have a clue how to answer her. She wanted to cry out that they'd shared a kiss and maybe, just maybe, the man wanted something more in a woman than a size two hardbody.

Kirsten just shook her head and shrugged and asked if she could refill the woman's glass.

Nikki handed her the empty wineglass.

Always the cool one, always the one to solve everyone else's problems, Kirsten brutally shoved aside her hope and went to get the refill. She got to the kitchen door just as the Jeep pulled up in front of the house. Seth was back. And with a bunch of partying guests that Kirsten knew she had to attend to whether she wanted to or not.

"So how can I get a personal assistant just like you, Ms. Meadows?" Rick Conway asked, his wolfish grin disavowed by the twinkle in his green eyes.

"You can't," Seth interrupted, giving Rick a quelling glance as he passed him on the trail.

Kirsten wanted to laugh. They'd been on the trail for an hour. Rick, another model named Skya and a broker named Bob, who clearly had the hots for Skya, rode together with Seth and Nikki. Kirsten had been asked to lead the group, since she knew Hazel's trails better than the ranch manager.

Rick pulled his quarter horse alongside Sterling. "But on the slim chance Mr. Morgan isn't paying you a fair salary for your—ah—services, Ms. Meadows, you know you can always—"

"Ask for an increase," Seth barked.

Rick laughed. "What is she? Your employee or a shareholder?"

"Why don't you harass Nikki instead, you dog." Seth smirked.

"Yes, why don't you harass me, Rick—sexually is preferred," Nikki chimed in from the back of the trail.

Kirsten cringed at the jab to Seth, but he didn't seem to notice.

"Pardon me, my lady." Rick took off his cowboy hat and bowed his head to Kirsten. "But if I'm to be sued for harassment, I'd much prefer Nikki's lawyers than Seth's. Alas…"

He reined in his horse and left for the rear.

Kirsten giggled. Rick was funny, but what made him hopelessly charming was the fact that he made fun of himself even more than others—an unusual trait, she figured, in the mega-ego world of stockbrokers.

"I should have warned you about him. To him, his whole life is one big party." Seth pulled Noir up alongside Kirsten's horse.

"He's fine. Not a problem." She stole a glance at him.

Seth looked like one of the cowboys who worked on Hazel's range. He hadn't shaved, and dust from the trail coated his hat and jaw. From beneath the brim, he met her gaze with a shadowed stare.

She wished she could say that he didn't wear the dirt and grime well, but deep down she had to admit he looked even sexier than when she'd first seen him in his immaculately tailored business suit.

"After dinner we'll be going into town for a drink," Seth said. "I figure you might like a night off before the barbecue."

She nodded. She'd seen her mother and sister only once since she'd returned to Mystery from New York. "Thank you."

He looked as if he wanted to say something more, but then thought better of it.

Then suddenly, as if angry at himself, he jerked Noir around and loped toward Nikki.

Kirsten didn't look back. Instead, she began a monotone travelogue of historical tidbits about the valley for the benefit of Bob and Skya, who looked as if they couldn't care less. But she cared, and she continued motoring her mouth uselessly.

Anything to keep her mind off the boss.

* * *

Carrie, Kirsten's sister, sat next to her on the couch, curled up in her arms. The eleven-year-old recounted the latest inexplicable fashion fad.

"And then you clip your hair up with these glittery ponytail holders and that's it."

"I'm exhausted—and you plan on doing this to your hair every day?" Kirsten asked with a smile.

"But it'd be really cute on you," Carrie offered.

"Not as cute as on you."

"Dinner's ready."

Kirsten looked up. Her mother stood by the living-room door, dressed in a denim shift and sandals. For the first time in ages, Kirsten thought, her mother didn't look tired.

"Retirement agrees with you, Mom," she said, hugging her. "I can't remember the last time I didn't see circles under your eyes."

"Nonsense. I'm going back to work just as soon as my hair's a little longer." Jenn Meadows smoothed the baby-fine hair coming in around her face.

"Viola keeps her hair real short. A few whimsical pairs of earrings and you'll look great."

"Who's Viola?" Carrie asked.

"She's Seth's housekeeper," Kirsten answered.

Her mother looked at her quizzically. "Seth?" she asked.

"Mr. Morgan," Kirsten added hastily.

In a move of self-preservation, she changed the subject. "Now that I've got the income, I just wanted you to know that I called about buying this place, Mom. I think I'd be so much smarter to just own this old cottage and quit throwing the money away on rent."

"But you don't even live here, honey," Jenn protested,

Kirsten winked at Carrie. "Yes, but you and Carrie live here—and who knows, Mr. Morgan may go out of town for months at a time. I might be back here more than you think."

"I don't know about that. As soon as I've had a rest, I'm looking for another job."

Kirsten sat at the table, grateful to be home if only for the evening. "When you feel up to it, Mom, you can get another job, but doesn't it feel great to know you can go out there and do something you'd enjoy rather than just something that's going to pay the rent?"

Jenn seemed overtaken with emotion. She was quiet for a long moment, then she took Kirsten's hand and squeezed it. "That would feel wonderful, darling, but you have to promise me you feel that way about working for Mr. Morgan.

Otherwise, if I found out you were miserable just to pay our rent, I don't know what I would do.''

''I love my job, Mom. Really.'' Kirsten gave her a smile and quickly turned her attention to her dinner.

There was no way she was ever going to tell her mother about all the complications. In fact, looking at her mother so rested and content, Kirsten only became more determined to make her job less complicated.

She could do it, too. It would take some discipline. She'd have to rid herself of daydreams. But she could do it. Besides, in all probability, Seth would get bored with Montana and go back to New York for long stints. That would make it easier. And who knew. He and Nikki might make up and get married. That'd solve all the complications.

Heartsick, she began to eat her dinner, unaware of her mother's scrutinizing looks throughout the entire meal.

''There's the girl Friday right now! And hey, it *is* Friday!'' Rick Conway jumped into Kirsten's path on the sidewalk.

After dinner she'd walked downtown from her mother's place so she could check on a few details before the barbecue tomorrow. James was

one of those dangling little knots. She wanted to
have a promise that he wouldn't act up if he was
going to play with the band. But she couldn't
get anywhere now with Rick blocking her path.

"Hello, Mr. Conway. I see you've been enjoying Mystery's many authentic saloons." She
wrinkled her nose at the smell of whiskey on his
breath.

"This place is fantastic. There's a good old
cowboy bar on every corner."

She smiled. "You don't have to try them all
tonight—just a little tip, being a native here and
all."

"Why so formal? I know you're not as cold
as you'd like to be. I mean, c'mon, you get all
my jokes. How cold can you be?"

The earnestness on his face made her laugh
aloud.

"See what I mean?" He took a staggering
step toward her.

"Did your companions abandon you, Mr.
Conway? Would you like me to call Jim to take
you back to the ranch?"

"Naw. They're right behind me. Just having
another spat. So what'd you do to that guy? He's
really upset Nikki—I told her she could bunk
with me tonight if she's as lonely as she says
she is."

"I—I—haven't done anything," she stammered, his drunken comment catching her off guard.

"He's got his radar on you good. So good." He snorted. "And that damn beautiful Nikki can't seem to figure out that the other woman's right under her perfect nose."

"No—no really—" Kirsten protested.

"No—really," he mimicked, then sobered. "Let me tell you, you seem like a nice woman. Seth's one cold jerk, and Nikki's just made for him. Just make sure you don't get yourself hurt." Rick leaned forward and whispered, "But if you do, I'm here. I'd love to comfort you, if you know what I mean."

She stared at him, unable to form any words. Rick's brazenness shocked her, terrified her even. She didn't want to be in a position to have to rebuff one of the boss's friends. But worst of all, his words about Seth's radar renewed the hope that she was bent on killing.

"Thanks for the advice," was all she could say before Nikki appeared, alone, sullen and demanding.

"What are you doing in town, Kirsten?" the model snipped.

"I had the night off. I thought I'd take care of a few details for the party tomorrow." She lifted a manila envelope she held in her hands, stuffed with papers. "So much to do, so little time."

"Well, we're heading back. We'll see you tomorrow."

"Without Seth?" Rick squawked, letting the model take him by the arm and lead him away.

"He wants to stay and I want to leave," the model announced, her every word laced with resentment. "Here are the keys to the Jeep. Do I have to spell it out for you, you lucky boy?"

Rick's eyes widened.

"C'mon."

He followed Nikki down the street like a puppy dog.

Kirsten watched them go.

She would even have laughed if she hadn't turned around and smacked into the hard, unyielding chest of her boss.

Five

"Looking for your ship, Miss Meadows?" Seth inquired, his tone sarcastic.

Cool and collected, she didn't let him ruffle her feathers. "I was in town and thought to check on a few details for tomorrow, Mr. Morgan."

She refused to take his bait. Clasping the manila envelope and her handbag, she made to walk around him on the sidewalk. "So, if you'll excuse me—"

"Tomorrow is a fait accompli. Take the night off." His words were like a military order.

"I think everything should go very well to-morrow, but I still have a few personal errands to run—"

"Personal errands. What kind of personal errands do you have to run at this time of night?"

She stared at him, exasperated. "I can certainly see why you've done so well for yourself, Mr. Morgan, but bullying me will get you nothing but…"

She paused for the right words, but there were none. There wasn't anything she could threaten him with. Quitting would only hurt her at this point in her life.

"But what, Miss Meadows?" he taunted.

"My—my—my displeasure," she retorted.

Even she had to laugh. She sounded like some nineteenth-century schoolmarm.

Grinning, he stared down at her while a couple of drunken young men rolled out of the Roundup Bar and came their way.

Not in the mood to tangle with tourists, she said, "Unless you have a task you need done, if you'll excuse me, this is my only time to take care of what I have to do in town. I've got to go."

"How are you getting home?"

"I don't know, sir."

He laughed out loud. The wolfish grin enticed

her and the spark returned to his wicked eyes. "You still can't walk around town alone all night. I'll go with you—for protection only."

The drunken men passed by, one accidentally staggering into her. The manila file flew out of her hand and the young men walked on, oblivious.

"You need protection, Miss Meadows," he confirmed as he bent and helped her gather the papers.

"Fine. Come along if you have nothing better to do than cause my displeasure," she told him, flustered as she tried to retrieve all her papers.

"Believe me. Your pleasure is the only thing on my mind, Miss Meadows."

She eyed him, glad they were underneath the dim street lamp and not in naked sunlight where she might read all the lust she suspected was in that last statement.

Giving up on conversation, she walked across Main Street, where the saloons were located, to Aspen Street, where most of the businesses had their offices.

The blocks were dark and desolate compared to the rowdiness of Main Street in the height of the tourist season, but she didn't mind. There was virtually no crime in Mystery. It really was pointless for Seth to come with her. She wondered why she hadn't insisted he go his own way and she go hers, but then she forced herself not to study the motivations too closely, because she didn't really want the answers.

She stopped in front of a plate-glass-fronted office named Mountain Mortgage.

Placing her entire file in the night box, she made a display of dusting her hands of it, then said, "Okay. Mission complete. My bodyguard can breathe easy once again."

"Are you buying a house?"

"Maybe," was all she offered.

"Why do you need a house when you live at the ranch?"

"Because this is a free country, and employees may do anything they like after work hours, including buying property the boss may not understand that they need."

She lifted one eyebrow and gave him a chastising look. "Does that explain it for you?"

"No. No, it does not. Does Hazel know you're buying a house?"

"I'm going to tell her if I get the loan."

"I know you think I plan on being in New York a lot, but I'm telling you right now, Miss Meadows, that I plan on spending most of my time in Mystery, and I'll need an assistant at my quarters, not living in town."

"I'm aware of that, Mr. Morgan."

"Then answer me. Why are you buying a house?"

"I'm buying it for my mother and sister, okay?" she finally snapped.

Her shoulders sagged, the stress of the past couple of weeks weighing her down. "Look, I just thought now that I had a pretty good job I should buy the cottage my mom lives in so she doesn't have to pay rent any more."

"Why can't your mom buy her own house?"

"Because she's been sick and worked to death. She needs a break, and I'm going to give her one."

A muscle in his jaw bunched as if he were pondering her words.

Tears suddenly stung her eyes. She didn't know how she was going to handle James at the barbecue tomorrow, and handling Nikki for the past two days had taken its toll emotionally. Right then, all she could think of was that she wanted to get away from Seth Morgan as fast as she could. She wanted to lick her wounds and quell her embarrassment and sort out her lacerated emotions alone.

She turned to leave, but he pulled her into the darkened doorway of the mortgage company.

"I'll buy your mother the house. You don't

have to worry about that,'' he whispered as if suddenly aware of her desire for privacy.

"I can't let you do that,'' she protested, her throat thick with tears of exhaustion. "In fact, I won't let you do it. It would be improper and perhaps even unethical.''

"I want to do it.'' His hands cupped her face.

She couldn't see his eyes in the darkness of the doorway. She couldn't tell if he was the Seth Morgan of substance or style at that moment, and she wasn't about to trust herself either, not when his strong touch sent an erotic rustle down her spine like the scattering of aspen leaves.

"It would take too long to pay you back,'' she said, the tears beginning to well in her eyes, her strength for protest dissipating.

"Don't pay me back, then.''

She looked up at him in shock. He stared down at her, his expression urging.

Soon the tears streamed down her face and onto his knuckles, which caressed her cheeks.

A strange moment held between them.

Her exhaustion and despair were getting the better of her, and she knew it. It was getting harder and harder to think with his warm touch on her face.

But he seemed undone by her crying. His face was a hard mask of marble, his eyes shadowed and piercing. She knew he wanted something, and it was frustrating him being unable to figure out how to go about it.

Slowly, he drew his tear-dampened knuckles across her mouth.

Her emotions raw, she was aware that now was not the time for a kiss, because she knew she couldn't protect herself from her protector.

But the kiss came anyway. And in the end, she wasn't even sure who kissed whom first. All she did know was that his lips were on hers once more, feeding her soul. And she held his mouth to hers as desperately as he held on to her.

Moaning, she allowed the kiss to deepen. His tongue licked fire into her mouth, and his arms trapped her like a cage as they moved around to her back and crushed her to him.

The want built in her like a pressure cooker. When his hand slid between the buttons of her blouse, she had no thoughts of pushing him away. She thought only of giving him more and more until she had satisfied her own growing hunger.

Another button popped open, then another and another. His hands were experienced at undressing a woman; their warmth and dexterity was enticing. Slowly he slid down her bra straps, leaving her breasts barely held in the pink lace bra cups.

As if she was weightless, he pushed her against the plate-glass door, his hands eagerly taking their fill of her generous female flesh.

She swore she heard him groan, but her heart beat so hard, she couldn't discern any other noise. His lips took hers in a taut, intense kiss, and she felt her very being meld with his with just the union of their mouths.

Breaking the kiss, he let his tongue trail down her tearstained cheek to her neck. He licked the sensitive hollow of her throat, burning her and leaving her only with a need for more fire.

Her breath came fast when she felt his thumb caress the lacy line of the bra cup along her breast.

His mouth hardened as if he was somehow trying to hold himself back.

But it seemed no use. His hand slid between her jean-clad thighs and roughly caressed her, as if readying her, as if she needed readying. All it would take was his mouth on her nipple and she would be his.

"Don't worry about that house again, baby," he whispered, his breath an erotic musk on her skin.

His words rained down on her like needle-sharp hail.

With an intake of breath, she suddenly seemed to snap awake.

She saw with crystal clarity what the hell she was getting into.

He was going to help her buy her mother's house, all right, and the price was going to be way more steep than the mortgage company's. And it might even take longer to pay. And the worst of it was, she had just about done it.

Just about.

Quickly she covered her breasts with her hands as they nearly fell out of her bra.

Trembling, she pulled out of the doorway.

"What happened?" he snapped, his own urges clearly setting him on the razor's edge.

"N-nothing. And nothing ever will happen. Un-understand?" she stammered.

"That's not the message I got," he shot back.

"Well, you got the wrong message, got it?" she said defensively, the tears streaming down her face once more.

He actually seemed dumbfounded.

"And I don't need you involved in my personal business." She backed away, her hands still covering her chest. "I plan on working for you because this is the best job I can get right now, but you need to know I want other things out of life—*other things*—''

''The house wasn't enough?'' he interrupted, all his acid cynicism filling each word.

She stared at him, unable to comprehend that a short walk could produce such emotional damage.

''Are you forcing me to quit? Is this where this is going?'' she asked, defiantly wiping her tears with the back of her hand.

He released a cold laugh. ''Yes, Miss Meadows, this is the rich guy's diabolical plan, don't you see? I get the whole blasted town to come to my ranch for a barbecue tomorrow with you running the show, and I force you to quit the night before the fiasco. Brilliant, isn't it?''

He walked up to her and roughly buttoned her shirt. ''Let's go,'' he said, taking her arm.

''Where?'' she asked, heartsick and exhausted.

''Back to the ranch. You've got a lot of work to do tomorrow for me, Miss Meadows.'' He gave her a caustic glance, one that sent a shiver of fear through her bones. ''And if you plan on continuing as my employee, don't forget that I demand perfection.''

''I can handle perfection,'' she answered in a small but cool voice.

He looked at her. His face lit up beneath the
street lamp on the corner, and she swore he took
her words as a challenge. The expression on his
face was filled with smirking doubt, and the light
that gleamed in his eyes gave no assurances.

She looked away, stumbling as she tried to
keep up with him.

Certainly she could handle perfection.

But the flawed, magnificent male animal that
he was—well, even she had to admit she had her
doubts.

Six

JJ James and the Outlaws played a lively two-step, children chased each other through the elated crowd, parents ate spareribs and there wasn't a cloud in the deep azure sky.

"It's the best danged Mystery BBQ Sizzle we've ever held," Hazel declared, the cattle baroness with her usual noblesse oblige drinking a beer in a bottle like her own cowhands behind the bandstand.

"And it's the last one I'll ever put together," Kirsten announced, her emotions still raw from the night before.

Hazel took a long, hard look at her leaning against the tent pole. "Something wrong, missy?"

Kirsten shut her eyes, exhausted. "Hazel, believe me, the last thing I want to do is look like an ingrate. As usual, you've done too much for me. I mean, you even helped with Mom's medical bills, but..." She sighed. "I don't know. I think I'm in over my head with this crowd. I don't understand any of them."

"All you've got to understand is your boss, Seth Morgan."

"I know. I know," she affirmed. "And yet he's the one who's the most confusing."

"Is he giving you mixed signals? Now, why would he do that, do you think?" Hazel suddenly came to life like a bear who'd found honey. She all but rubbed her hands together in glee.

Kirsten almost laughed. "Nope. Trust me. The signals are all too clear."

"Well, what kind of signals are they?" the old gal demanded.

A terrible thought suddenly occurred to Kirsten. "Hazel, this job—I mean—you didn't plan on this being some kind of matchmaking scheme, did you?"

"Certainly not! What kind of friend do you

think I am, cowgirl? You said you needed a better job, and I figured Mr. Morgan's offer ain't hay, so I threw you to it.''

Hazel did an excellent job of looking affronted. In fact, Kirsten almost believed her.

''It doesn't matter, Hazel. I'm not accusing you of anything. Nothing's going to happen between me and my boss in any case, because I can guarantee it won't. But with that issue aside, the job is still difficult.''

''How so?'' Hazel took another beer from the cooler, looking suddenly a bit deflated.

''It's just—well, it's just that when Dad left, I knew I wanted more out of life than what my mom had. She settled for something less than love for the lifestyle and security, and she ended up with nothing. I'm not doing that. No matter what. It's all or nothing for me.''

''Good girl,'' Hazel confirmed.

''But this Wall Street crowd.'' She shrugged. ''I'm out of my element. I don't understand any of them. It's so easy for them to go from bed to bed. Nothing means anything to them, not even love. I guess when you have so much to fall back on, you don't need life to mean anything— but not me. I just don't work that way.''

''Sounds like this is turning into more than a

job to me," the cattle baroness prompted, her Prussian-blue eyes suddenly aglitter.

"No. It's just a job. I guarantee you." She studied the older woman. "But I do want to know one thing, Hazel. Why did you sell to him? I mean, of all the people in the world who'd love a piece of your ranch—why him? What made him so worthy?"

The cattle baroness took a long sip of her beer. She seemed to contemplate her words good and hard.

"You know me, Kirsten. The best way I can explain it is I've never been able to see a person go a-wanting. I couldn't let him go a-wanting, either."

Kirsten gasped in disbelief. "Wanting? The man wants for nothing. Nothing."

"It wasn't the land he wanted. Hell, he could have gotten a ranch anywhere. And I didn't have to sell to him. You know that. I've sent bigger wolves than him back to the city with their tails between their legs after they ask to buy me out."

"Then why?" Kirsten asked, nothing making sense now.

Hazel met her gaze. With a wisdom that was beyond even her seventy-plus years, she said, "Sometimes a person can go a-wanting most when he has everything. Sometimes city folk are the loneliest people on earth, but it's not from having no company—too much company there, if you ask me. That's why I'll never leave Mystery."

Kirsten wondered if she understood. "Are you telling me it's something bigger than the land Seth wanted?"

"Maybe. What do you think?"

She wasn't sure.

Her hesitation and uncertainty must have shown on her face, because Hazel said, "He's only your boss, cowgirl. You don't have to answer the question, just work for him. In fact, I'm wondering—just a little, mind you—why you want to know all these things?"

A sly smile tipped the corner of the cattle baroness's pretty mouth. "Unless, of course, you want to figure him out—but then there go all your guarantees, right out the barn door with the pony."

"Hazel, you're wicked, you know that? Just plain wicked." Kirsten nudged her. "But then, you haven't gone up against Seth Morgan either, and I don't see your schemes working there."

"Never underestimate age and treachery, my dear." The famous blue eyes winked at her. "I make eight seconds every time."

Kirsten laughed at the woman's bull-riding metaphor.

The only thing she could think to say next was, "Gee, I'm way overdue for a drink."

Grabbing a cold beer, she left Hazel to her machinations and surveyed the crowd once more to see if anyone needed anything. The band was on break, but the crowd seemed to have enough ribs and cold drinks not to notice.

"Kirsten."

She turned around, surprised to find James standing there. He was staring at her, a hungry look in his brown eyes she knew all too well.

"Band on a break?" she asked, hiding her surprise beneath a pleasant tone of voice. "You guys really sound good, by the way."

"I didn't look you up, girl, to get your opinion of the band. I want to know how the hell you are." He crossed his arms over his chest.

She smiled, another ploy to cover her nervousness around him. "Fine. Just fine. And how are you?"

"Wondering why we aren't married by now," he answered sourly.

Inwardly she groaned. When she'd hired the band to play for the barbecue she'd hoped they wouldn't have to go there. "I thought we'd settled this—"

"You aren't dating anyone else here in Mystery. So why not me?"

"How do you know I'm not—"

He interrupted her again. "I know. I'm from this town, remember? My friends keep me informed."

Exasperated, she said, "Well, your friends might be wrong. Thought of that?"

He grabbed her hand and tried to pull her to him. "C'mon, little lady. You just think you're better than everyone else here 'cause you went to fancy schools and all, but deep down you know I'm good enough. Maybe even too good."

She closed her eyes, desperate to keep her temper. "James, we discussed this. We're just not right for each other—"

"Is this not right?" He bent to kiss her.

She pulled away.

He tried again.

"No. I said no," she protested, trying to wrench her arm free.

Suddenly he was pulled from her and thrust aside like so much trash.

"The lady said no," Seth growled, his sea-colored eyes as frosted as his expression.

"And who the hell are you?" James shouted, his temper flaring.

"I own this place, that's who I am. And you happen to be manhandling my employee."

Suddenly James's eyes narrowed. He looked Seth up and down, assessing him. Then he turned to Kirsten and spat out, "Ah, I get it now. You refused me 'cause you knew there were greener fields out there, didn't you? And everyone in town knows your kind just like 'em green with money. That's right, green with money, not like our fields that just have good old honest Montana grass."

He bent and picked up his straw cowboy hat that had fallen off when Seth shoved him aside.

He gave her one long poisonous look and said, "So long, Kirsten. When he divorces you, or better, never marries you in the first place, give me a call sometime. If I'm not busy, I'll see if I can fit in an extra bronc ride or two for you."

He stomped away, glaring at Seth.

Seth didn't give him another look. Instead, his gaze was fixed on Kirsten.

She opened her mouth to protest, to refute, to say anything that would prove what James had said wasn't true. But every denial seemed so pointless.

She covered her face with her shaking hand. After a moment she resumed her usual cool demeanor and said, "I'm sorry you had to hear that. James and I dated for a while. I guess he's still sore it didn't work out. I had hoped hiring him for the barbecue wouldn't turn into a scene, but I guess I misjudged him."

Seth said nothing. His hard, cynical expression said it all.

Those same old tears stung her eyes, but she would be damned if she'd let him see her cry again. She was not out for any man's money, but there was no way to convince Seth Morgan of that when every woman he'd probably ever known knew the worth of his bank account and never bothered to assess the worth of his character.

But that was beside the point now. She and Seth Morgan would never have a romance. They were doomed from the beginning because it was love she wanted, and if she had to look long and hard to find it, if she had to marry a man who mowed grass for a living, she'd do it. Good old Montana grass was fine by her as long as it came with a kind, honest man who loved her.

"Your ship came to say that I'm leaving for New York tonight. I've had a crisis at work that can't wait. The guests can stay here until my return, but I'll need you to get out some faxes before the plane takes off."

His words contained nothing but dry, accusatory indifference.

She withered inside. Just looking at him made her ache. He thought she was something she wasn't, and he had every right to in his situation, and there was nothing she could say to convince him otherwise.

"I'll be right there, Mr. Morgan," she whispered, her voice hoarse from withheld tears.

"Viola has the stack of papers. See that it's done."

"Yes," she choked out as she watched him turn and leave, her heart shattering.

The party was over—a great success if the attendee count was correct.

Staring out across the fields next to the house where the barbecue had been held, Kirsten sipped on a chardonnay, feeling very much like Nikki at that moment.

Gone was the wide-eyed wonder of her kiss with Seth in the stream. To Seth, she was now right up there on the list of models and actresses and women who prowled the Wall Street scene just to catch themselves a millionaire.

She could tell by the expression in his eyes that she'd now been reduced to gold-digger status.

And no matter how hard she thought, there seemed no way to change that image.

But worse than that was the fact that he was now doubly dangerous to her heart. If before he was dabbling with her, discovering what she was really like, there had at least existed the possibility he might find something that he could respect.

A relationship with him was doomed. She would never be anything more than Nikki was to him, and despite her jealousy of the model, Kirsten didn't want the same relationship with Seth that Nikki had. No, she wanted her own, on her own terms. She was not like Nikki, who when things didn't work out with one man would just hop in a different man's bed. Kirsten was almost certain Nikki had spent last night with Rick.

Now that the barbecue festivities were over, she couldn't wait for the houseguests to leave, but she didn't set the schedule—Seth did. And he was making no effort to have his New York buddies return home.

Reminding herself over and over again, she told herself she had to have this job. If she feared there was even the remotest possibility that she might fall in love with Seth, she knew she would have to leave. It would prove a disaster to everyone. Just everyone.

But mostly it would prove a disaster to her. Because she knew in her heart that if she ever fell for Seth, she would fall hard, and there wouldn't be a place on this green earth that she could go that would exorcise him from her heart. And then, like her own mother, without even knowing love she would be finished with it. Forever.

She glanced down at the empty wineglass. Feeling downright morose, she watched Nikki and Rick romp in the pool, cooling off after the hours in the sun at the barbecue. Their laughter chilled her, and the only thing she could think of that might help the hole in her soul was another glass of wine and a long, bitter soak in the bath very far away from anything relating to Seth Morgan.

Seven

Kirsten was surprised by Seth's quick return. He was back in twenty-four hours. She was even more surprised by his foul mood. However, he wasn't any worse for the wear, because of his private jet.

"I want all of the letters cc'd to Mary, and I want the originals for my files," he dictated, his imperious self sitting at the large oak desk in the living room.

He reminded her of a gruff old bear, one that had a thorn in his paw. Kirsten wrote carefully, making sure she got everything he told her.

"And I want—" he growled.

She squelched a giggle.

He drilled her with his stare. "Is there something funny, Miss Meadows?"

She adamantly shook her head. "Nothing. Nothing at all, sir."

But it was a fib. She found even their conversation ridiculous. They spoke like two strangers when they were not strangers at all.

The more irritated he looked, the more she wanted to laugh.

"Please share the joke with everyone, Miss Meadows."

Her self-control melted. He'd sounded like her junior high school geography teacher.

"Forgive me, I've just got a case of the giggles, I guess." She hiccuped, holding her mouth tight against any further laughter.

He assessed her, his expression dour. "When you're through with this, that will be all for the night."

She stood. "I'll get it done right now."

"Fine." He dismissed her and watched her go, those icy eyes hooded and inscrutable.

She went into the utility room where the office machines were hooked up. Within ten minutes she had written the memos and faxed them. When she returned to the great room in order to go upstairs for bed, she saw Seth through the large windows. He had already mounted Noir and was going down the road at a lope.

He was taking an evening ride—without her.

She swallowed her annoyance and resentment.

Her feelings were entirely irrational, she told herself again and again. Her status in the household meant she held fewer rights than Viola, and she certainly didn't see the housekeeper pining to go for an evening ride with the boss.

Depressed, she went to her room, bathed and slipped on her comfortable old flannel robe. Thinking she might borrow a book from the great room, she walked downstairs, made herself a cup of hot tea in the kitchen and went to find a book to take upstairs.

Nothing interested her. The books were all dry-as-dust tomes on the bond market.

Disappointed, she sat down on the couch, sipped her tea while it was still hot and made a pledge to go into town the next day and buy some novels and magazines.

Chilled, she sat closer to the fire still burning in the large fieldstone fireplace. Curling her bare feet beneath her on the couch, she made a mental note not to get too comfortable.

She didn't want to stay too long. Seth would be returning any minute from his ride, and she didn't want him to catch her cozying up by the fire. *His fire.*

But the tea warmed her, and soon her thoughts drifted. Unable to summon the energy to crawl back up to her bedroom, she closed her eyes for a few seconds, just enough to regain her momentum.

Before she knew it, she was fast asleep.

Dust laden and worn-out, Seth walked from the stable to the house in only the moonlight. Jim had been waiting for him and had taken care of Noir.

It'd been a long ride, and both man and beast needed a rest.

The galloping had been good for Seth. He'd needed the burst of energy. It was better than anger, more satisfying, more healthy. In truth, it gave him equilibrium.

When he'd tiredly dismounted, he'd realized that Hazel might be manipulating the situation, but her manipulations were just that. If he so chose, he would forgo the ranch and find a place elsewhere. He didn't need to be the cattle baroness's puppet.

But his frustration was caused by more than just Hazel. Kirsten frustrated him. He was nothing more than a means to an end for her.

Granted, she'd made that clear from the beginning. Her mother was ill and needed care. But it infuriated him to know she viewed him no differently than had the rest of the bank-account gold diggers who'd been after him in the past. He wondered if he would ever find a woman who could see the man behind the money machine.

But her less-than-sterling motives didn't take away the fact that he had a wicked attraction to her.

Perhaps he was drawn to her merely because she was good at hiding her true motives. If he hadn't overheard her on the phone talking to her mother about their ship coming in, and if he hadn't heard that old boyfriend of hers confess to what a climber she was, he suspected he'd have fallen for her, fallen hard. She seemed to be everything a man could want in a woman—she was smart, graceful, feminine. She had a come-hither look he'd first seen in the jet, and it was so well rehearsed that she seemed completely unconscious of how it had been manufactured to drive a man crazy. And more important, when they were alone and not under the guise of ''work,'' he felt somehow that she saw him. *Him.* The man, not the bank account.

He pushed open the heavy pine front door to

the house, his cowboy boots softly clicking on the flagstone.

Before him, in the great room, she lay on the couch asleep, as enticing as a fairy-tale princess.

Her blond hair formed a halo around her face, the wheat color glistening with gold highlights from the fireplace flames and the rich background color of the burgundy sofa.

She lay slouched back against the pillows, her frayed, raggedy pink flannel robe parted slightly, playing a sweet game of peekaboo with the lush, generous curves of her breasts.

He stood stock-still for a long moment and just stared at the picture, unsure whether he should reprimand her or go to her and slip his hand deep inside the part in the robe.

Slowly he walked up to her.

She didn't move. Her breathing was deep and even, her face an angel's in repose.

The whole thing was a setup. It was so obvious. Fall asleep in the ranch's great room, and then when the seduction was through, make a great gesture of dismay at how he'd taken advantage of her.

As he bent down to the sleeping beauty, he wondered what she wanted out of it.

Kirsten would want more than just a little jewelry, he had no doubts about that. And maybe that was what made her so powerful. Unlike any other woman he'd ever known who was happy with just an account at Tiffany's, Kirsten wanted more. She wanted his soul.

Kirsten sensed the feather-soft caress on her cheek well before she felt it. In her dream state, nothing seemed real; everything was accepted. Even a touch could morph into some crazy plot that made sense only to the dreamer.

The stroke came again on her cheek.

Fluttering open her sleepy eyes, she looked and found Seth, his face so close a kiss was only a breath away.

It seemed as natural as rain to let him kiss her then. He knelt by the couch like a prince. The fire licked golden light across both of them, urging them on, drumming the rally call to their primal instincts.

She wasn't dreaming. He was truly there, kissing her, taking her chin in his hand, his other hand slipping familiarly between the part in her flannel robe and squeezing her breast.

Neon signs should have flashed by then, telling her she was getting in over her head.

But the warnings never came.

Perhaps she was lonelier than she admitted even to herself, perhaps she was truly falling in

love with him. She didn't know. All she did
know was that she'd woken from a beautiful
dream only to find the dream had substance. Her
deepest, darkest fantasy was coming true and
leading to a nightmare. And she had no power
to fight it. No power at all.

He slipped out of his shirt and cowboy boots.

She lay on the couch watching him with
heavy, need-filled eyes. When he unzipped himself out of his jeans, her breath caught. He was
more than she'd bargained for, and yet her
thighs quivered with the harsh emptiness between them.

No words were spoken. The understanding of
the moment was upon them.

He tugged on her frayed flannel belt and
pulled the robe aside, revealing all of her. By
instinct, her hands went to her chest, but he
pushed them aside, taking in every detail like a
man who'd been starved.

His mouth caught her large hardened nipple.
The sensation made her delirious with want. His
hand roughly cupped her other breast, and he
moved to that nipple, unable to get enough of
her.

Her hands swept down his chest. The cool
night air made his nipples hard and flat, but as
he lay atop her, his back warmed by the fire, his

body was a delicious study of temperatures. Cold and hot—just like his eyes, just like his expression.

He kissed her, his teeth nipping at her tongue, his own tongue licking fire down to her soul. His hand stroked her face, then her vulnerable throat, his thumb sweeping the hollows with dark, sensual sweeps.

His passion, however, was nothing less than white-hot. He groaned his readiness, his hips grinding instinctively into hers. She drummed the rock-hard muscles of his waist, driving him on to the end they both knew was coming. Cradling his head in her hands, she proved her own hunger by allowing him to sink between her thighs.

Before she could take in another deep kiss, before she could breathe in his scent of horses and leather, he dived deep inside her, filling her to gasping.

With any other man she might have protested the swiftness, the totality of his possession. But there was nothing to protest when her willingness to surrender transcended his plundering.

He moved against her, slowly at first, his face mirroring all the sensations that she drank in. But soon his hunger got the best of him. His demanding nature won. He pulled on her lower lip with his teeth, his tongue thrusting in and out of her mouth much like his manhood, tempting, promising, fulfilling.

Her desire built until she was at the precipice, his every movement painful in her need to hold back.

But then the dam broke. Grabbing the arm of the couch, he slammed himself inside her as if he wanted to crawl in there himself. He groaned her name against her hair, his hips grinding possessively into hers.

She tumbled into his honeyed oblivion. Taking all he had to give, she held him to her, her last coherent thought the terrible possibility that it had all been a dream. And would be no more.

Eight

The phone rang on her line. Thinking it was her mother, Kirsten rolled over in her bed and picked it up, her voice groggy with sleep.

"Kirsten? This is Ms. Halding from the mortgage company."

"Of course." Kirsten became wide-awake.

"There's a problem."

She tried to focus her sleep-puffed eyes on the receiver. "I don't understand. A problem?"

"Yes, well, it's the strangest problem I've ever encountered in the thirty-five years I've worked in mortgages—"

"What is it?" she asked, frustration constricting her chest.

"Your financing has been rejected, Ms. Meadows. The title company researched the loan as a purchase, and they've put a halt to it. I'm sure there's been a misunderstanding. I told them you weren't double-dealing anyone, but I have to admit, in their defense, it does look fishy."

Kirsten felt as if she were in a bad dream.

"I—I don't understand," she stammered, sitting up in bed, suddenly aware she had no nightgown on. "I applied for a mortgage. The owner of the property agreed to sell—"

"But the title company came back and said you already own that property, Ms. Meadows. You bought it cash. The title's in your name. You can't purchase a property you already own. However, if you really just wanted to cash out, I can get you in touch with our equity arm...."

The room seemed to spin.

The woman's voice dwindled to background noise.

"Did you hear me, Ms. Meadows?" the woman asked again into the phone.

"Yes," Kirsten croaked. "I guess I'll have to get back to you. Thanks for trying, though."

She put down the receiver.

A flood of memories of the night before rushed at her like a freight train.

Chagrined, she recalled the hours on the couch, how she'd wanted more, and then more, and how Seth had given her everything she wanted until they'd both fallen asleep, spent, in each other's arms.

Somehow he must have carried her to her bed, because she didn't remember waking and going to her room. He'd spared her the embarrassment of Viola finding them on the couch, but she couldn't help but feel a twinge of disappointment to wake alone in her own bed after a night of such soul-piercing abandon.

Now she was going to have to deal with the realities of her irresponsibility. The realities and the consequences.

Stumbling to the shower, she knew she was in trouble when she didn't want to step into the hot spray.

His scent clung to her hair and body like rare perfume. She didn't want to wash him away. The musky male scent was stirring, even comforting to her senses, but life had to go on. Obligations had to be met. Denials that their night meant anything to her had to be made.

She slathered shampoo in her hair, closed her

eyes and scrubbed. The shower did revive her, and the cleansing renewed her good sense.

She would have to face him like his personal assistant and no more.

The first thing she had to do was to confront him about her mother's house and tell him how she would pay him back.

She was still rattled that he'd bought the house right from under her. She'd asked him to stay out of it, begged him not to get entangled in any way. Now she was in it up to her ears.

Refusing to think he'd orchestrated the house purchase just to get her into bed, she decided the timing wasn't right. Besides, just the thought that that was what had happened would make her too angry.

And, in the end, leverage hadn't even been necessary.

Now she just had to be sensible, get out an equity loan and pay him back. Then the fact that they'd had a little sex wouldn't hurt so much. It wouldn't leave her so vulnerable and hoping there might be more.

Comforting herself, she knew she could be the queen of denial. They'd had a little sex, and it was no big deal. It meant nothing. No obligations on either side.

She closed her eyes and let the water run

down her. Of course, she was fooling herself. Their night together had been the kind she would comfort herself with when she was old. Indeed, she'd finally known what it was like to be fully a woman, to make love with a man who neglected neither body nor soul.

A small moan escaped her lips. They hadn't used any birth control. There might be repercussions beyond just the two of them.

It seemed unimaginable that she could have Seth's child, but it was a possibility. Nature was something that had a will of its own. And if she did become pregnant, she knew she would have the child. He would be very much like Seth, yet untainted by money and cynicism.

She shook her wet head, letting the drops spray across the marble tiles.

No, starting now, she was the queen of denial. She wouldn't think about all the consequences right now. She just really needed to focus on what she was going to say when she saw him next, how she would act, how she would smile and shrug off the most magical night of her life as no big deal.

Queen of denial. Queen of denial, she kept repeating to herself like a chant.

She saw Seth out in a paddock working on one of his barrel racers. Coolly observing his expertise on the quarter horse, she walked up to the fence and perched on it.

He spied her and loped toward her.

"Howdy, ma'am," he said in his best cowboy accent. He took off his hat to her.

She smiled. He always looked particularly roguish and handsome in jeans and a flannel shirt.

Losing her control, she imagined how wonderful it would be to have come to the paddock, given him a kiss and told him how much last night had meant to her....

Queen of denial. Queen of denial.

She let the smile freeze on her face. "I just wanted to see if you had anything you needed me to do. I have to go to town this afternoon. To take out an equity loan to pay you back for Mom's house."

"Don't bother." He studied her, his eyes hooded beneath the straw brim of his hat.

She shook her head. "I told you, I can't accept the offer. It's out of the question."

"I thought now was different. I mean, after last night I really don't see the need to pay me back."

His words cut into her heart like a dull, serrated knife.

He clearly thought she'd slept with him to get the house. She'd told him she wasn't about to pay for it with her body, but from his point of view, he'd ponied up the cash and right after he'd paid, there she was, waiting for him on the couch, as pliable and complicit as a spoiled mistress.

Choosing each word with care, she answered, "Last night changed nothing. I will pay you for the house."

"Changed nothing? Or meant nothing?" he demanded gruffly.

"Of course it meant something. I had fun—didn't you?"

Her tone was light, her words breezy. Inside she was anything but that.

She couldn't believe the conversation. It was breaking her heart. But she had to remain collected. She had to save herself.

Queen of denial. Queen, queen, queen...

"Fun?" He repeated the word dully, as if he didn't understand it.

"Look, I want to be gracious about the house, but I can't accept the help, and I *will* be paying you back. I don't want any strings. I said that before, and I'll say it again—no strings."

His face took on a rock-hard cast.

She could have sworn he said, "Holding out

for more, huh?'' but before she could ask him to speak up, he simply nodded and cantered away.

Heartbroken, she was dismissed.

Three days passed. Three days of living hell as far as Kirsten was concerned. She and Seth were barely on speaking terms. Desperately she wanted to demand why he was so closemouthed, but she was afraid of facing the answers as much as she was lonely and confused.

Worse than that, she needed her job now more than ever in order to pay back the huge loan she was taking out on ''her'' house. If she were fired, there was no way she could manage those payments.

Frustrated, she told Viola she was going to take Sterling for a little exercise. Seth had gone to town, and he'd left no work for her to occupy her time.

The mountains always worked to clear the mind and free the soul. Determined to cleanse both, she took off toward the high country, the late-afternoon sun slanting red-gold lacquer onto the granite face of Mount Mystery and the Continental Divide beyond.

Choosing the horsepacker's trail in order to find solitude and really think, she loped Sterling easily through the foothills, her thoughts as dark as the thunderheads in the distance.

She had to get over Seth.

It would be difficult, to say the least, but she had no business falling for him in the first place. He was way too powerful to wrangle with, and even if she could make demands on him, he would never bend to her terms. The warning signs had been fluorescent, and she'd wilfully ignored them. He was a rich man, used to manipulation and getting what he wanted. The sale of her mother's house proved that. She was out of her league pretending she could be his match, out of her league in thinking he could be more than James or her father, men who viewed women as compliant dolls. Men who rebelled at the first sign of will in a woman.

Her gaze grew clouded. Even the beautiful stag that jumped through the field ahead of her didn't take her mind from her woes.

But that she was falling in love with Seth was without question. The other night had only cemented her growing feelings. Certainly she was no virgin, but the night with Seth, even on the confines of the couch, had meant more than all her lovemaking experiences combined.

But loving him wouldn't make him love her back. And there had never been any talk of love with him. His cynicism with Nikki was enough to make Kirsten never, ever broach the subject. She knew she wasn't strong enough to take the answers.

She got to the steep path that ultimately led to the pass and the Continental Divide. Guiding Sterling expertly along the narrow rocky ledges, she was so immersed in her thoughts, she barely took notice of the rain until heavy plops of water began to pockmark the dust on the trail ahead.

The wind picked up. The sun hadn't set, but it might as well have, given the opaque black clouds that hid it.

Sterling held her ground even when a spider vein of lightning cracked across the sky, followed immediately by earsplitting thunder.

"What a gem you are." She soothed the animal, patting Sterling's dappled neck.

Kirsten knew if she headed back to the ranch she'd just get soaked and perhaps even break Sterling's leg in a mud slide, given the storm's sudden downpour.

Her better judgment told her to ride it out. There was an old miner's lean-to along Blue Rock Creek. It was still ten minutes away, but it was the best she could do under the circumstances.

Turning Sterling around, she headed down the path to Blue Rock Creek.

"Viola, I'd have thought you'd have gone to bed by now. I've never seen you up this late. You're pacing like a caged bobcat. What's wrong?" Seth asked, having come down from his suite to pour his own coffee from the coffeemaker on the kitchen counter.

Viola looked hesitant. Her gaze flickered from the storm to her boss.

"What's going on?" he demanded.

"I don't know, sir. I don't know what to think. Maybe I should inform Jim—"

"This is my ranch. So tell me."

"I'm sure everything's all right." The woman hugged herself and stared out at the storm that lashed the kitchen window.

"What is it?" Irritation sounded in his voice. From his expression it was clear he would brook no more wavering.

"It's just that Kirsten decided to take one of the horses out. Now with this storm, I'm a little worried she didn't get in yet." Viola smiled, but it didn't budge the worry in her eyes.

She waved aside her anxieties. "Oh, I'm sure she's stuck having to listen to Jim's tall tales in the barn.'' Her gaze slid to the window and the wall of water that pummeled it on the other side.

Seth picked up the phone. Pounding in the speed dial, he barked into the phone, ''Did Kirsten and Sterling get back yet, Jim?''

The grim silence gave the answer before he hung up the phone.

His thoughts tortured him. She couldn't be in danger. He wouldn't allow it. He cared too much. He realized he'd gone too far to lose her now. *And he would not lose her.*

Viola returned to staring at the window. ''I know she's an experienced rider and Sterling's a reliable mount, but still, I'd hate to think of her going through this on top of the mountain.''

Seth was already pulling on his slicker.

''I'll be happy to call for help from Hazel's ranch, sir, to look for her,'' the housekeeper offered.

''I'll find her,'' was all he said before he donned his black felt cowboy hat and headed out into the storm.

Nine

Kirsten shivered against the lean-to. She was at least out of the rain, but the temperature had dropped severely and she was soaking wet. Chunks of ice rained down on the tin roof.

It had to be forty degrees now, and when she'd left, the late-afternoon temperature had been almost eighty. She hadn't even taken her polar fleece. Her only covering was a wet pair of jeans and a T-shirt.

Huddling next to Sterling for warmth, she tethered the animal while it ate what little straw was left from the last person who'd occupied the three-sided shack.

The storm would pass and she would be on her way soon, she told herself, her teeth chattering so loudly she could hardly hear the thunderous rain and hail pounding on the corrugated tin roof.

She hadn't told Jim where she was planning on riding, but there was no point in wondering about that, because she didn't need a rescue party anyway. She just needed the rain to end so she could safely see her and the horse's way home.

Slowly lowering herself against the side of the cold metal lean-to, she hugged her knees and wiped the water from her face.

It would be only a matter of minutes before she could be in the saddle again and heading home.

Just a matter of minutes, she told herself, a strange feeling of comfort and warmth overtaking her thoughts and tingling through her soaked and freezing body.

And her mind was feeling sleep run through it like a narcotic. Maybe just a little nap would warm her....

When Seth found her, he could see hypothermia was taking over. Kirsten hardly roused when he shook her. Her lips were a bluish color and her clothes were soaked through. She had nothing on but a T-shirt and jeans in the forty-degree weather.

He tethered Noir, quickly took a blanket from his saddle pack and pulled aside his slicker. Treating her like a rag doll, he tore off her wet clothes, bra and panties and all, and pulled her cold nude body against his chest, covering her with his own chamois shirt and the blanket.

"I'm—all—all—right. I—I—I'm all r-r-right," she protested groggily, her teeth clacking away as she spoke.

"When you're warm we'll get back to the ranch. Until then, just relax." His arms encircled her farther, wrapping her as close to his body heat as possible.

"Why did you take my c-c-clothes off?" she stammered.

"You would have frozen."

She looked up at him with those dark blue eyes that drove him so wild. Prudishly she said, "You really shouldn't have, you know."

He chuckled.

Tiredly she leaned her cheek against his chest.

"You know," he mentioned wickedly, the rain still pounding the sides of the lean-to, "the professional wilderness rescuers would recommend that we have sex right now. It would really get your blood flowing quickly.''

Her hand shot up. She took a weak kitten swipe at him, but missed altogether.

He laughed and tucked the slim chilled arm back inside the chamois shirt. ''I guess you're warming up just fine.'' He slouched against the cold sheet tin siding.

Wrapped up together, they waited for the rain to end.

''I'm fine, Dr. Saville. Really I am. I just didn't know the storm was going to be so severe.'' Kirsten sat up in her bed. The handsome young town doctor had been waiting for them when she and Seth had arrived back at the ranch, having been called by a frantic Viola.

Mortified at her state of undress when she'd dismounted—Seth hadn't allowed her to put on her wet clothes—she had gone right upstairs with Viola, shrugged out of Seth's chamois shirt and steeped in a hot bath.

Now, with a bowl of hot chicken noodle soup in her belly, all she really wanted was a nap and some privacy.

''Hypothermia's nothing to fool around with, Kirsten. Everyone thinks it's the snow and ice that will kill you, but more people die from cold exposure above thirty-two degrees than below. The body can't get warm while wet.'' Saville wrote out a couple of prescriptions. He gave them to Viola.

"I'll check on the patient in a few days. Call me if she seems to be coughing or catching a cold.''

Viola nodded.

Kirsten thanked him. "And how is Rebecca?'' she inquired politely about his wife.

"She's due the end of September. Number two, you know.'' His face flushed with pleasure. "I don't know how she does it. She's a miracle worker.''

Watching him go, Kirsten wondered if her own husband would be so totally in love and devoted to her as Saville was to his wife.

Dr. John Saville and his wife, Rebecca O'Reilly, had been the talk of Mystery during their courtship. The rumor mill had it that they were one of Hazel McCallum's famous matches. So far it had proven to be a blazing success.

Kirsten slouched back in the pillows.

Tomorrow she was going to have to begin again with her boss; she would have to forget that he'd rescued her from sure death, forget that every kiss, every caress was like food to her hungry soul. Seth Morgan had become less and less like a boss and more and more like a lover.

Yet she was fooling herself that she could ever manage a detached attitude. They'd gone too far. They'd been through too much.

And besides, she was in love with him.

She almost laughed piteously with the thought of it. Yet it felt good to admit it. The queen of denial was dead. It was like the old saying: Now that there was no hope, she felt much better.

He would never return her love as she required it. He was too rich, too powerful, too controlling. He wasn't the kind of man who could raise a passel of children and look forward to making love to his wife, night after night, through a lifetime.

Sighing, she closed her eyes, exhausted. She hadn't realized how fighting cold could wear a person out.

Within seconds she was fast asleep, nestled beneath her eiderdown comforter, dreaming she was wrapped in the warm steel arms of the man she loved.

Seth stoked up the fire in Kirsten's bedroom fireplace. Viola had gone to bed, but he couldn't without first checking on her.

He stepped over to the mound curled up in the middle of the large pine bedstead.

Leaning over, he listened. Her breathing was even and clear. A golden twist of hair peeked out from beneath the comforter. Lovingly he stroked it, amazed at its silky texture.

She moaned and turned beneath the covers. A hand slipped out, perfect and feminine.

He fought the urge to squeeze it, to make her aware he was there. Right now she needed to recover. She could even have died out there if no one had found her.

The thought made him physically ill.

Straightening, he realized how much he'd changed in the few weeks since he'd arrived in Mystery. The old superficialities had no lure for him any longer. Now all he wanted was a warm fire and a good woman. Kirsten. Forever. And ever.

He looked down at the sleeping, vulnerable woman.

He was thinking too much. That was certainly not him where women were concerned.

Maybe Mystery really was changing him. Or maybe it was his friendship with Hazel.

Or maybe it was the beautiful girl asleep in the bed.

All he did know was that the financier in him

couldn't accept failure. And yet Kirsten Meadows was dangerously close to having the power to make him fail. His sure thing, his money, seemed to hold no sway with her. And so he was left bare, unable to understand what might win her.

With that dark thought he silently let himself out of her bedroom and went right for an ice-cold shower

Ten

――――

"**E**veryone's made too much out of yesterday. I'm fine. Really. Just embarrassed." Kirsten blushed answering Seth's inquiry into her health.

"That was foolish of you to go alone," he said, looking ominous even while he relaxed on the couch. *Their* couch.

She handed him the current faxes and opened her laptop. "I just wanted a ride. I won't do it again. I realize it was a terrible inconvenience to you. I'll ride at Hazel's from now on."

"If you want to ride the horses here, I just insist that someone go with you. You know the trails better than Jim does, but the ranch manager here's an experienced mountaineer and you're not. I don't want to ever hear of you going out alone again.''

He gave the faxes a cursory study.

She watched him, thinking he looked less rested than she'd ever seen him.

Against her better judgment, she wondered what had kept him up last night and wished desperately it had been a longing for her.

But that couldn't be. She'd made a total fool of herself yesterday. And even if she hadn't, his words at the paddock the other day had made it clear that their relationship was based on sex and money, and nothing more. She could never go along with that. She wanted love, and not even a skyscraper would be an adequate substitute for it.

Viola came out from the kitchen. ''Your mom's here, Kirsten—oh, am I interrupting?'' She looked at Seth.

Seth scowled. ''We're finished.''

As was his manner, he went back to his faxes.

Kirsten left the room with Viola.

''Mom!'' she exclaimed once she got into the kitchen.

She made the formal introductions between her mother and Viola, then made her mother comfortable at the huge pine table in the middle of the kitchen.

Viola poured some soda while Kirsten chatted with her mother.

"You look great, Mom. Love the earrings," she added, thinking the whimsical flamingos at her mom's ears not only flattered the pink in the woman's cheeks, but also made her short hair look chic.

"So, does Carrie like the art camp?" Kirsten chattered on. "I always thought she had the talent in the family."

"She wants to make jewelry, so she's definitely got the expensive talent in the family." Jenn Meadows rotated her head slowly, modeling the earrings. "These are your sister's creations. Not bad, eh?" She laughed, then accepted the soda from Viola.

"Well, I've got Jim waiting for my opinion on the pool flower beds, so I'll leave you girls alone to visit." Viola left through the kitchen door, but not before asking to buy a pair of Carrie's earrings.

At last Jenn turned to her daughter. "You, on the other hand, young lady, don't look too well. Are you eating right? Are those dark circles I see under your eyes?"

Kirsten wasn't sure how much to tell her mom

about yesterday. Dismissing her appearance, she said, "I had a long day yesterday, that's all. But I'm fine. Really."

"Is the boss working you to death?"

Laughing, Kirsten said, "Hardly. In fact, I have so little to do, half the time I think he should let me go and save his money."

Her mother winced. "I hope that doesn't happen. But if we need to sell the house to take care of that mortgage, I'm ready. I'm really starting to feel great. The relaxation is doing me a lot of good." A furrow developed between her brows. "But you know, Kirsten, you should never have bought the house. It's one thing to give me a rest—it's another to take on too much responsibility."

Right there was another thing over which Kirsten knew she hadn't bothered to go into detail with her mother.

"Look, the house is good for you, and especially Carrie. I can afford it, so let's not talk about it again." She looked down at her soda.

"Fine. But promise me one thing. You'll come to dinner tonight for a housewarming. Carrie's had me shopping and cooking all day so we can show you our 'new' home."

"I'll have to check with Seth—" Kirsten

closed her mouth. "I don't know why I said that—I meant Mr. Morgan."

At that terrible moment Mr. Morgan walked into the kitchen.

Her mother stood up to greet him, a smile beaming on her still-beautiful face.

Kirsten made the introductions. "Oh, there you are, Mr. Morgan," she announced nervously. "Mr. Morgan, I'd like you to meet my mother, Jenn Meadows."

Jenn extended her hand and smiled more.

Seth shook it warmly.

"It's so nice to finally meet you, Mr. Morgan. We were so excited when Kirsten got the job," she said.

The old hardened cynicism was written all over his face as he glanced at Kirsten. He clearly remembered the conversation that first night when Kirsten had declared that her ship had come in.

"She's been invaluable to me here. I'd have to go back to New York constantly without her taking care of things on this end," he added with unusual graciousness.

"How kind of you to say so." Her mother's smile broadened.

"I hope you don't mind my visiting with

her?'' Kirsten asked. ''She lives in town and just came out to see me for a minute.''

''Take all the time you want,'' he answered.

Her mom piped in. ''I just came to invite Kirsten to the house for dinner. We're having a housewarming for her, Carrie and I. We just purchased the house we live in.''

''Really? Congratulations.'' He looked coolly at Kirsten.

Kirsten's heart stopped. The last thing she wanted her mother to find out was that Seth had bought the house outright for them. That would open so many floodgates, she wouldn't live long enough to close them all.

Desperate, she tried to change the subject. ''If you haven't got much for me to do this evening, I'd like to go to dinner with my mom and sister, but of course if there's work to be done, we can always make it another time. Right, Mom?''

''Certainly,'' her mother enthused.

''There's nothing for you to do tonight. Go right ahead.''

He stood there, not moving. Eventually he leaned against the granite counter, proving to Kirsten he was enjoying her discomfort way too much.

''Well, th-thank you,'' Kirsten stammered.

"D-do you need anything right now?" she asked him. "Otherwise—"

"Of course, we understand that you might have other plans, Mr. Morgan," Jenn interrupted, "but we'd love to have you come to our little celebration, too, wouldn't we, Kirsten? After all, it seems only proper to have the boss to dinner every now and then."

Kirsten froze.

There was no way she could get through a family dinner with Seth at the table.

Convinced he'd decline, she tried to hide her nervousness behind a pleasant smile. "Mom, I'm sure Mr. Morgan has better things to do than accept our last-minute hospitality."

"I'd love to. What time and where?" Seth announced.

Kirsten just stared at him.

"Oh, about seven. And the address is—"

Kirsten had had all she could take. "Mr. Morgan can get the address, Mom. We'll be there."

Jenn grabbed her handbag and keys from the kitchen table. "I'd better be going, then. Lots to do before company arrives!" she said before breezing out the kitchen door.

When her mother's car was safely out of sight, Kirsten turned to Seth and said, "It was very gracious of you to be so kind to my mom, but really, you don't have to come tonight. I mean, it won't be fancy or anything. Our idea of a feast is pizza.''

''Don't you want me to come, Miss Meadows?'' Those aqua eyes of his laughed.

''Of course you're welcome to come, but I don't see how you'd ever have a good time—''

''Don't worry about my good time.''

She stared at him, speechless.

''Will you be ready for six-thirty?'' he asked.

''Yes,'' she answered, sure somehow she was being set up, but not quite seeing the scheme.

''How do you dress for dinner at your house, Miss Meadows, if I may ask?''

''Pizza casual.''

''Do I detect sarcasm?'' He lifted one dark eyebrow.

She studied him. None of it made sense. Unless he just wanted to check out the property he'd bought.

''You know,'' she mentioned, ''you can see the house any time without having to sit through a family dinner. And I am paying you back, so really you won't have anything to do with the property as soon as I get the loan I've applied for.''

''You've made all of that perfectly clear, Miss Meadows. Now if you'll excuse me, I have to go down to the wine cellar and pick out a nice bottle to bring to your mother.''

She watched him open the door past the kitchen table. There, with its own staircase, was the wine cellar.

''Red or white, Miss Meadows?''

She rolled her eyes. His motives always caused suspicion in her. Perhaps it was just wisdom. He was not the kind of man one could control. But he had to know that ultimately he would not control her, either.

''Whatever you like,'' she offered, her voice sugar sweet.

''Then we'll bring both. Good choice.'' He smiled, then disappeared down the stairs.

A dinner had never taken so long in Kirsten's entire life.

Fearing any subject might lead to something she did not want to talk about, she stayed animated through the entire meal, so that she could turn the topic to her own liking should the need arise.

However, she needn't have bothered.

Her mom and Seth seemed to have taken an instant liking to each other. Jenn talked of all the places they'd lived overseas while Kirsten was growing up. Seth, the world traveler, naturally found it all fascinating.

Naturally.

But the worst one was Carrie. The preteen girl seemed to have taken one look at Seth Morgan and developed an incurable crush on the man. When Carrie showed him the jewelry she'd been making and he complimented her on her originality, Kirsten thought Carrie would swoon.

It was all too much. And too dangerous.

Kirsten didn't want her family attached to Seth, too. It was hard enough battling her own feelings after all they'd done together. She sure didn't want to answer to her mother's and Carrie's feelings, as well. It was too much like...

Well, it was too much like being entangled.

"Seth, have you ever been to the Devil's Elbow?" Jenn asked, serving dessert warm from the oven. "That's the old part of Mystery where Carrie and I picked these blackberries in the pie. It's not the most magnificent view, but if you walk far enough, you'll come to the old grist mill. You can swim there, and if you bring a bucket, you can get all the blackberries you can carry home."

"I haven't seen that part of the valley yet. I'll have to saddle up Noir tomorrow and take a ride out there."

"If you need someone to show you, I know how to get there," Carrie offered, her blond ponytail bobbing up and down in her eagerness to please their guest.

Kirsten tried damage control. "Surely, Carrie, Mr. Morgan doesn't need our—"

"Can you ride?" he interrupted.

The ponytail bobbed again. "Hazel taught me."

"I've got a good cob in the stable you can take. His name's Plat—short for Platinum. Looks just like your sister's horse, Sterling, only a hand or two smaller."

"My sister has a horse?" Carrie exclaimed, amazed.

"It's not my horse. Mr. Morgan just meant that I can ride her, but it's his horse." Kirsten suddenly realized she was exhausted. Monitoring conversation was worse than mountain climbing.

"Your sister's free to ride Sterling any time she wants," Seth said, accepting Jenn's second helping of pie. "And you feel free to come and ride Plat. I'll tell Jim, our ranch manager, that you have special permission."

Carrie looked at her mom, her blue eyes dancing with awe.

Being virtually fatherless, Carrie had had very

little male attention in her life. It made Kirsten's heart ache to see her so eager for Seth's attention. To be made to feel this special was something the girl was not used to. And Kirsten dreaded the moment when it might end.

"Well, that was a wonderful dinner, guys, but if you'll excuse me, I think I'm feeling a little under the weather so I guess I need to get going." Kirsten stood.

"So soon?" Jenn asked. "I thought you haven't been sleeping well."

"But what about our ride tomorrow?" Carrie added.

Kirsten didn't want to burst her sister's balloon, but these things, as she herself knew from personal experience, were less painful popped earlier than later.

"We'll have to see about the riding, Carrie. Mr. Morgan's a busy man. We don't want to inconvenience him."

"Oh," the girl said, suddenly deflated, as if realizing how foolish her enthusiasm had been.

"Miss Meadows, I want you to take me to Devil's Elbow tomorrow and I want you to have your sister come along, also. The boss, if you pardon me, has spoken." Seth's words were a command.

Kirsten was silent. No one was cooperating.

And there was only so much she could do to intervene if they didn't help her.

"Certainly, Mr. Morgan," she said, hugging her enthralled sister goodbye.

"Come back again soon, won't you, Mr. Morgan?" Jenn held out her hand. "We don't have anything too fancy here, but when you've lived everywhere in the world, you certainly know about hospitality."

Seth squeezed it. "I'd be honored to be invited again. Thank you."

They got into the Jeep, Kirsten silently fuming the entire way out of town.

"Your family's wonderful, Kirsten," Seth said in the dark car.

"Thank you." She didn't know what else to say. Her family *was* wonderful. Which was why she was so insanely protective of them.

"Did you know my parents died when I was in college? Car pileup on the autobahn in Germany."

"I'm sorry," she said, watching him.

He gave a wry smile. "Maybe we could have been a version of a family, but it would have required getting to know one another, and that wasn't something either of them wanted. In the end, I suppose it made it easier for me to adjust to not having parents anymore, since we weren't close.''

Silence permeated the car for a long moment.

Finally he added, ''You know, I always thought you couldn't miss what you never had. But lately I don't think that's true. I don't think it at all.''

She agreed, her voice soft with empathy. ''That kind of emptiness is far and wide. But when you've had something and it gets taken away, well, I've got to tell you, that emptiness goes pretty deep.''

Her thoughts spun to her father, and then to Carrie. The girl would get so worked up every time her father called that Kirsten and her mother had begun to wish he'd just stop calling.

Just the thought of it now made Kirsten realize she couldn't allow Carrie to get attached to Seth.

''So I guess if I sell the ranch back to Hazel, that'd be worse than never having had a ranch at all.'' His words seemed to come out of nowhere.

''Why would you sell the ranch back to Hazel? You just built it,'' she blurted out, confused.

''Hazel didn't sell me the land without attachments, Kirsten. There's always the provision that

I'll have to sell back to her if I don't meet the contract.''

"What do you have to do to meet it?"

He slid his gaze to her, then back again to the night road. "It's complicated. Something the lawyers drew up. I just don't know if I want to meet the provisions.''

"I see.'' She turned her focus to the road. The ranch gates lay ahead, an artful crossing and weaving of twisted pine.

The impermanence rattled her. Having moved so much as a child, having had her parents break up, she'd always longed for something she could count on. Now, when she worried about whether or not she and Seth Morgan should be lovers, she should have been more worried about what she didn't know, like his contract with Hazel.

Releasing a dark little laugh, she commented, "Life is so ironic. Just when you think you have everything by the horns, something comes up behind you.''

"What do you think you have by the horns? Me?'' he growled, suddenly becoming the confrontational Wall Street financier.

She shook her head, still smiling. "I'll never have you by the horns, Mr. Morgan, thank you very much.''

"What's that supposed to mean?" he demanded.

"Nothing. Nothing at all," she said, still laughing at herself and her pathetic little hopes that kept springing up despite how severely they were crushed.

The car stopped in the front driveway, and she got out. Walking toward the stables, she paused when he grabbed her arm.

"Where are you going? Not out for a midnight ride, I hope?"

Freeing her arm, she said, "I just thought I'd go for a short walk. Just some thinking time. Do you need me for something back at the house?"

"No," he answered.

"Then I guess I'm off. So I'll see you later."

She left him in the driveway, wondering if she had been a little harsh, but she was getting overwhelmed. If he sold the ranch, she'd have no more job. No house. No retired mom. No stability for Carrie.

It all weighed on her like Atlas holding up the earth.

She walked behind the stable to one of the short trails that led to a nearby meadow. There was a full moon, and the path was lit as if by electric lights. Once in the meadow, she sat along the hillside and watched the moon slide behind the mountains.

"It does clear your mind, doesn't it?" Seth said, taking a seat on the grass next to her.

She wasn't surprised he'd joined her. It was just like him, to read her thoughts, to sense her yearnings.

"How could it not clear your mind?" She lay back against the padding of grass on the hill. "You can't see those stars just anywhere. Those are Montana stars."

"Kirsten, I'm not a fortune-teller," he said, clearly something on his mind. "I can't see into the future, but more and more I realize how much I want to stay here."

"Sounds like the choice is yours," she commented.

"It's not all up to me. I've realized some things have to work out on their own. They shouldn't have a puppet master." He was silent for a long moment. "Do you understand what I'm saying?"

She nodded, tears stinging her eyes. Having been flung far and wide by her puppet-master father, she knew all about such things. Her family had been thrown to the wolves all in the name of her father getting his own way. But Kirsten also knew about living on the edge of chaos, when everything depended on a razor-thin edge of luck and there was not one damn thing she could do about it.

Seth was saying he might keep life as status quo. Or the roulette wheel would spin and he'd up and sell to Hazel, pay his accounts and leave town forever.

She would never see him again, because she never had any reason to go to New York. Their time together would be distilled down to a summer fling. One that nonetheless had changed her forever because she had fallen in love.

Pointing up to the sliver of moon that was still visible above Mount Mystery, she said, "If you leave, you'll miss that. That's a Montana moon. You can't get that anywhere else, you know."

He studied her in the moonlight, his eyes never lifting to look at the breathtaking display above.

Hesitantly he leaned over her.

His gaze locking with hers, he said, "You know what else is up there that I'd miss?"

She looked up at him. He leaned over her, his body fitting to hers like an old familiar lover.

With a yearning like none she'd had before, she desperately wished he would fall upon her, kiss her and make love to her beneath the stars.

"What else is up there?" she whispered.

He gently kissed her mouth. "It's up there and all around."

"What is it?" She moaned as he kissed and licked the sensitive hollows of her throat.

"It's a Montana heaven. A heaven like no other."

He poised above her, his weight held up by the corded muscles of his arms.

Knowing if she continued with him she would succumb, she nonetheless wrapped her hand behind his neck and pulled him to her.

In seconds they'd shrugged out of their clothes, using them as a blanket over the crush of fresh grass. The world smelled of spruce and male body heat.

Kissing him, she writhed beneath his chest, which covered her like an armor of warm steel.

Safe and secure for now, she opened herself to him fully. He tasted her as if she held nectar. Slowly, dizzily, she succumbed to his mouth, his ever-thrusting tongue. The moment built first in her belly, then, running her fingers through his dark hair, she allowed the fire to seep into her loins. It exploded with a force that made tears rush to her eyes. And made her gasp his name. *Seth.*

He silenced her moan with his mouth. His kiss tasted of blackberries. He filled his hand with her aching breast, then filled his mouth with her nipple. When she could take the exquisite torture no longer, he thrust inside her, and she found her release almost instantly. And then, as he continued, she found it again and again in rolling waves that seemed to have no end.

He alone made it a Montana heaven.

With Seth, it was the only heaven she'd ever known, and the only heaven she feared she ever would.

Eleven

The next week passed as if Kirsten was in a dream.

Despite her fear and hesitation, Kirsten decided to take one last chance and grab life with both hands. Carrie came almost every day to ride and she, Seth and Kirsten would take off to the horsepack trails of Mount Mystery.

Her little sister was completely entranced by Seth, his quick smile and generosity, but Kirsten couldn't blame her, when she herself was finding herself enslaved by him and her insatiable desire for him.

Nights were spent either in her room or his.

Viola had yet to guess their relationship, and Kirsten noticed both of them were reluctant to reveal it to the housekeeper. To do so would mean they would have to define the relationship somehow. They would have to admit it not only to the world, but to each other. That last night in the mountain grass had changed things somehow. A helplessness had seemed to overtake both of them. Their longings, their instincts, had taken over. But would it last? She tortured herself to find the answer.

There were barriers, and she knew it.

As she lay entwined in his arms one night, sated but unable to sleep, she thought of all the problems they faced.

She had a trust problem because her father had left, but Seth, too, had a trust problem. A woman was either a gold digger or out for sex. There were no other possibilities as far as he knew it. She didn't know if she could ever get him to see that there was more to life than money and carnal desires.

But she would try. She now knew she loved him enough to try.

A soft sigh emanated from her lips during her ruminations.

He opened his eyes and ran his hand down her cheek.

"After that long ride we had today, I'd have thought you'd be exhausted." He smiled, his face boyish from sleep.

"I'm just thinking about the day," she confessed, a wry smile on her lips.

His hand tightened on her bare hip. "I think Carrie had a blast. Especially when we took the horses swimming in the watering hole."

"I've never seen her have such a good time," she admitted.

He studied her. "Is there something on your mind? You seem so quiet."

She shrugged. "I'm great. So great that I wish the day had gone on forever and ever."

"Bull markets don't last forever. I know that better than most." He snorted. "That's why you have to make the most of what you have. Carpe diem. Seize the day."

"I think we did that today without doubt. And we seized the night, too," she added.

Smiling, he nipped at her bare breast. "I think we did, but it's hard to make every moment count when you're baby-sitting. Do you think we can do without Carrie tomorrow? Maybe we could take a picnic and climb McCallum Point?''

''I don't know, Mr. Morgan. You set a child's expectations, they have to be fulfilled.''

''But I've given at the office. Can't I have a day off?''

She released a bittersweet laugh. ''Oh, I see now—you have a greedy side. You want more?''

''I always want more,'' he growled, rolling on top of her, pinning her beneath him.

She looked up at him, her eyes filled with love.

But the confession gave her pause. It was silly to read more into it than what might have been meant, but she couldn't help herself. There was so much unspoken between them, so much unconfessed.

Overcome by the weight of her thoughts and the future, she instinctively turned to her side.

''What is it?'' he asked, his brow furrowing with concern.

Shaking off his question, she said, ''I had a great day. A wonderful day. Let's leave it at that. Why fiddle around with perfection? Why fix what ain't broke?'' she said, quoting Hazel.

"But what more is there?" he asked, his hold suddenly turning to iron.

"You know what?" She gave a dark laugh. "I don't know what more there is. Isn't that funny? I know there's more. I know I want it. But I don't quite know what it is."

"Where do you think you're going to find more?" he answered defensively. "You think just any man has what I have to offer?"

A hellish minute went by while she turned and stared at him.

All at once she blurted out, "It may shock you to discover this, but I'm pretty sure I could find happiness with a man of less means than you, Seth Morgan. And I can't help but wonder what you mean by 'offer,' because I know you have money. I've known it from the beginning. I'm your assistant, remember? But what more is there?"

She was silent for a long moment, her expression at once accusing and withdrawn.

"You know what?" she began slowly. "There is a lot more. And if this is all there is, I think you're giving it to the wrong girl."

"You didn't complain a few minutes ago," he rumbled ominously.

"So maybe you should give it to Nikki, because from what I could see, she was pretty darn happy with whatever you threw at her.''

A shield of ice went up in front of him.

Narrowing his eyes, he said, ''I don't know what's eating you all of a sudden, Kirsten, but if you don't see what I have to offer, then you're blind. Blind and foolish.''

She rose from the bed and slipped on her faded flannel robe. ''You do have a lot to offer, Mr. Morgan, but a couple of rubies and a new car isn't what I had in mind.''

She hated the fact that they'd gotten to this awful moment of truth, but it had come and she would have to give in to it.

''I'm sorry.'' Her voice was choked with unshed tears. ''I'm really and truly sorry.''

She thought of Carrie and the disappointment her little sister would suffer once she realized Seth's affections were as fleeting as Kirsten had thought they were. ''Yes. I'm sorry for everything,'' she repeated, tying her robe and leaving for her room.

''Carrie, I'm too busy to go riding today. Can I call you later and let you know what's going on?'' Kirsten held her breath. The morning had dawned bloodshot-red, and she'd seen every minute of it. It was now 9:00 a.m., time for her to cut Seth's ties with Carrie and time for Kirsten to go into her protective shell.

"I've got art camp at noon, so it's no big deal," Carrie said over the receiver.

Kirsten breathed a sigh of relief. "We'll work it out to go riding again, but right now just hang tight, okay? Love you," she rasped before hanging up the phone.

Sitting down, she realized all that she'd burdened herself with.

Her mother needed the mortgage paid; her sister had been promised another long riding lesson. Kirsten would never meet all her obligations while under Seth Morgan's power.

But he could make her live or die just by the wave of his hand. She was, in truth, nothing but a dispensable employee. He didn't need a personal assistant when Mary in New York could take over at a moment's notice and fill the job in the meantime.

She rubbed her eyes and realized the only way to save herself and her sister was to quit.

Seth had made love to her countless times, his soft words and kind deeds had touched her, and every gesture, every caress, had convinced her what she was seeing was real.

But he'd never said he loved her. He'd never offered a commitment. The wealth at his fingertips seemed to be nothing more than a manipulative tool.

His machinations would work with most girls. Most women were all too greedy for the next Porsche, the next trip to the jewelry store.

But truly, Kirsten was not Nikki. If she and James had truly been in love, she could have been the wife of a band singer. She could have lived the life of a roadie just to be near the man she loved, the man who loved her.

But Seth offered none of that. And she was in a dangerous game if she was going to hang around and try to convince herself there was more. If she continued down the path she was going, she would only drag Carrie and her mother down with her. It would be a catastrophe for all concerned, and her mother and Carrie had been through enough.

Startled, she looked up to see Seth at the front door. Sitting in the great room, she hadn't seen him come upon her.

"Jim is waiting to saddle up," he announced, his face taut with wariness.

"Carrie's not coming today. She has art

camp. Neither am I,'' she added hastily. ''I've got a lot to do.''

His expression as hard as honed steel, he said, ''I'm your boss, Kirsten. I don't remember giving you any work.''

She looked around the room—anywhere but at him. ''I've got personal errands to run if you don't need me.''

''Such as?'' he commanded.

Giving him an acid glance, she said, ''Believe it or not, I've got a life beyond you, Mr. Morgan. I've got to close on that loan for my mother's house, and I've got other personal matters to attend to.''

''What is it with you? Yesterday seemed to go perfectly. Now you act as if I forced you into my bed,'' he snapped.

''I don't want a contract for a relationship, okay?'' she blurted out. ''I want a relationship, not a benefits package.'' Despairing, she confessed, ''Look, let's face it, Nikki speaks your language. She understands what it is that you stand for. I don't, okay? I don't,'' she finished, depressed, and yet driven to speak her mind.

''What are you saying?'' He crossed his arms in front of him. Scowling in the open doorway, he looked like a marauder ready to strike.

"We've got to break this off before there's a lot of explaining to do to my mother, Carrie, Viola and anyone else," she said.

He looked furious. "You're an adult and so am I. Why do we have to explain to anyone?"

She knew he wouldn't understand. He was used to getting his own way, to manipulating people. He bulldozed emotion like most people ran over pavement.

But she knew she had to protect her own, even if she couldn't protect herself. It was one thing to disappoint her, it was another entirely to disappoint Carrie. She couldn't allow that to happen, no matter how painful it proved to be to her.

"I'm giving my notice, Seth. I can give you two more weeks, then you'll have to replace me." She looked at him, her usual cool facade covering up the volcano of emotion inside her.

"I don't take well to people telling me what to do, Kirsten."

She stared at him. "Well, this time you're going to have to, because you can't force me, Seth. I'm not a robot. I'm not a slave. More than that, I'm not a fortune hunter who will do your bidding with just the lure of a shiny object. No, Seth, I'm a flesh-and-blood woman who wants more out of life than you have to offer. So I'm getting out of here. I'm going to see what else there is in the world for me.''

She stood and made to leave.

''I don't think I've ever met a woman I couldn't figure out, but I can't figure you out, Kirsten. Not at all,'' he told her, his voice bitter.

''You can't figure it out, Seth, because it's too simple.''

She gave him one last lingering look, then with tears in her eyes she ran up the stairs to her room.

Twelve

———

When Kirsten saw the New York tabloid the following week, her world stopped. After her announcement that she was quitting, Seth had taken off on his plane to New York. She hadn't heard from him in a week.

Devastated, she told herself over and over again that the parting was for the best. After all, he surely hadn't mourned it. Instead, he'd taken off for greener pastures, if the headlines didn't lie: Fab Financier Seth Morgan to Wed Supermodel Nikki Butler. Wedding Plans Secret, Strictly On The Q.T.

Heartsick, she shoved the paper aside and sank into her misery.

As if she could read Kirsten's mind, Hazel was on the phone a minute later.

"What's all this nonsense in the paper about your boss?" the cattle baroness demanded without even a greeting.

"I guess he's getting married," Kirsten answered dully.

"You mean you're his personal assistant and you don't even know the story?" Hazel snorted.

"He left for New York a week ago, Hazel. He doesn't report to me. He's my boss, remember? I report to him."

"And you haven't reported to him in a week? Darlin', you're to report to him this instant. This instant!"

Kirsten wanted to laugh, but the unshed tears choked her.

"He's my boss, Hazel, but he's not going to be that for long. I'm sorry to tell you this after all the effort you went through to get me the job, but I've handed in my notice. I've only got one more week to go."

Hazel was silent, as if absorbing the information. The sympathy in her next words shocked Kirsten.

"You mean you've only got one more week to endure. Isn't that right, my dear?"

Despite her self-control, Kirsten burst into tears. "Is it that obvious?" she cried.

"I'm an old polecat, dear. You can't fool me when I've spotted someone in love."

Kirsten wiped the tears running from her eyes. "I don't know how it happened. It just did. Maybe deep down I wanted it to happen, but I thought I took every precaution…every precaution…."

"You're pregnant, too?" Hazel gasped. "I'll kill him."

"No, no, no." Kirsten sniffed. "Well…at least I don't think so. But that's not really the point. I'm a big girl, Hazel. I knew what to do, and somehow I did everything wrong. I knew he was all wrong to get involved with, and now I'm going to have to live with the consequences of my foolishness. *All* of the consequences, if need be."

"You want to come live with me at the ranch while we sort this all out, cowgirl?" Hazel offered.

"I told him I'd give him two weeks' notice, and I'm going to do that one thing right if it kills me." She sniffed again.

"He doesn't deserve that," the cattle baroness said in condemning tones.

"Maybe." Kirsten brushed at her wet cheeks. "But it takes two to tango, and I jumped, Hazel. With my eyes wide-open I made the stupid decision to jump."

Hazel McCallum met this news with a far-from-defeated sigh. "Don't you worry, dear. Things have a way of working out. There's still time."

Kirsten laughed darkly. "Yes. There's one more week. And if I'm lucky he won't invite me to the wedding."

Another day passed before Kirsten saw Seth.

He arrived like any other time, quietly, in his Jeep. She was sitting before the great-room fire on the couch where they'd made love. Before she could rise from her seat, the door opened and he was there, looking as handsome and devilish as he had ever looked.

"Ah, Miss Meadows. Fine. I'll need you to alert Viola that we're to prepare for fifty visitors for next Saturday." It seemed to be work as usual for him as he shrugged out of his suit jacket and went to his desk to survey the faxes for the day.

Kirsten couldn't believe the stab she felt in

her heart at seeing him. The very idea of him marrying Nikki left her ill. As Hazel had foretold, she would have to endure the last moments with him, but seeing him now, knowing he was lost to her, suddenly seemed more than she might be able to take.

"How was your flight?" she inquired, her cool facade coming to her rescue.

He looked up from his desk.

Warily he replied, "The usual."

"Congratulations." She forced herself to meet his gaze. She would have her breakdown in private, but in front of him she would never reveal her devastation.

"You wish me well?" He seemed almost taken aback.

"If Nikki brings you every happiness, then I must." She said nothing else. There was no more to say.

He studied her for a long time, his sea-ice eyes searching, probing. "Kirsten, I've decided to stay here in Mystery, to keep the ranch. Come hell or high water, I want to stay in Mystery."

"If you're hell-bent on staying in Mystery, then do what you must," was all she offered.

She herself would not be staying in Mystery. Not with him around. She had roamed the world before when her father had been with the diplomatic corps. If she had to do it again to find her place, then she would drag her mother and Carrie along for the ride. Anything to get away from Seth and the pain in her heart.

She gathered up the book she'd been reading in front of the fire. Departing, she said, "I'm sure we'll be busy the next few days, so if there's nothing more, I'll see you in the morning." Numbly she made for the huge staircase to the side of the great room.

He stared after her, not speaking, his expression full of unnamed emotion.

"Kirsten." His jaw bunched. "I—" His mouth jammed shut.

"Yes?" she asked, her breath shallow and anticipatory.

"I—I hope you sleep well."

He roughly dismissed her with his cool glance.

Wounded anew, she simply nodded and went to her bedroom.

Only when she was alone did she release her despair, rubbed raw by the renewed hope of seeing him again. She wept silently, her only succor the fact that the clock was ticking, and soon she would see him no more.

"This is the strangest thing," Mary said to Kirsten discreetly into the phone from New

York. "Nikki Butler is burning up his lines of credit all over this town to get ready for this wedding, but it makes no sense why he wants to transport all that to that ranch to get married. Especially when she hated that place. Positively hated it. It's all over town how she loathed that visit," the executive secretary confessed.

Kirsten closed her eyes, not wanting to hear any more details.

Finally she offered, "Perhaps he's the one who likes it here."

"Precisely my point," Mary said into the speaker. "If he's so in love with her that he wants to marry her, why do it at a place she can't stand? I'd have thought he'd sell the place, she hated it so much. At least, that's what all the gossips have to say about it."

"Men. Don't try to understand them, Mary. They'll drive you insane," she attempted.

"But," the secretary continued in her conspiratorial voice, "I have a theory. I think he's been involved with someone up there. I think he wants to get married there just to prove a point."

Point taken, Kirsten thought to herself bitterly.

Point so taken it had pierced her heart and ripped it out.

In a modulated voice Kirsten said, "Seth Morgan has the world at his fingertips. Why would a man like him bother to make a point to someone? Especially a point so extravagant?" *And futile,* she added silently.

"I don't know why. All I know," Mary went on, "is that I've worked for the man for over fifteen years. I know him as well as my son and husband. I was with him through the loss of his parents and through the building of his empire...and something's gotten to him, I tell you. I wish I could say it was Nikki, but I just don't see it. I don't see it at all...."

"What do you need me to do?" Kirsten asked, desperate to change a subject that was getting all too close to her.

"Well," Mary mused, "Nikki called, and she said the wedding gown designer will have to do the final fitting in Mystery...."

Kirsten didn't hear a word Mary was telling her.

Like an automaton, she took notes and offered appropriate uh-huhs when necessary. Her mind, however, was miles away, kissing her lover midstream in the creek, seducing Seth on the couch, licking her heart wounds as she forced herself to emotionally prepare to leave him.

"I'll get it prepared," she said to Mary when they were finished.

"Hey, are you all right?" Mary asked, innocently inquisitive. "Your mom's still doing okay? I've been dying to come up there. I can't wait to meet all of you at the wedding."

Kirsten gave a choked little laugh. As if she would put herself through that ceremony.

"Mom is doing spectacularly."

"Good." Mary sighed. "You know, I've gotten quite fond of you, Kirsten. Seth has told me how much you've done for your mom. You deserve the best."

"Thank you."

Kirsten didn't think now was the time to spring it on Mary that she would be leaving in less than a week. Besides, the wedding would speak for itself. Her absence would be noticed by some, certainly Hazel. If Mary put two and two together, she would realize why Kirsten didn't attend the wedding, and there would be no need to explain further.

"Oh, and by the way, Nikki will be calling you," Mary advised. "And she's been Catherine the Great ever since that diamond went on her hand, so beware."

Mary said goodbye.

Kirsten hung up.

Suddenly in her heart of hearts she realized the whole charade was a losing game. There was no way she was going to advise Nikki on her wedding gown. Enough pain was enough, and she was no masochist. Her promise to stay the extra week was null and void, given the latest maelstrom being thrust upon her.

She went to find Seth and tell him the truth—that she would be leaving right then.

But the damnedest thing was, she couldn't find Seth anywhere.

He wasn't out riding Noir, and he hadn't summoned the plane. Without friends in town, he never took the Jeep, but the vehicle was missing just the same, and even Viola said he'd made no mention of needing anything in town.

Frustrated, despairing and trapped, Kirsten did something she never did. She went to the wine cellar, retrieved the most celebrated bottle of champagne there and popped it open in the great room on their couch.

"Do you love her?" Hazel's question shot out as if she was a detective grilling a suspect.

Seth sat in the McCallum parlor, upright on the century-old mail-order settee, looking more uncomfortable and belligerent in Hazel's presence than he'd ever been.

"You said I needed to settle down. I'm doing that. Is love in your sales contract, too?" he parried.

"I'm looking out for your best interests here, cowboy, so don't cross me. You can't marry this twit Nikki Butler. She's all wrong for you. You'll be miserable."

"The tabloids say it's the match of New York."

"Well, here in Mystery we have a different standard of matchmaking, and you and Nikki Butler won't make the grade—let me inform you of that right now," Hazel retorted.

"Why not?" he taunted, his jaw set, his long muscular form dwarfing the settee.

"Because you love Kirsten, and dadgummit, I've never been wrong about these things." Hazel stared at him like an angry badger. "She's your match, son, and if you don't mind my words, you'll pay by losing her forever."

His eyes went subzero. "I am not about to admit an indiscretion with an employee, Hazel."

Hazel snorted. "All this employee-boss political correctness is nothing but cow pie in this case. I don't believe it, and the sooner you admit to loving her, the sooner you can grab happiness with both hands."

Seth seemed to ponder her words long and hard.

Finally he said, "I'll admit Kirsten is unlike any woman I've ever known."

Hazel seemed to sense the chink in his armor. Craftily she said, "I'll make you a deal, son. Look me in the eye like an honorable Montanan, and tell me you don't love Kirsten Meadows. If you can do that, the ranch is yours, and your marriage is yours to do with what you want."

She studied him with her notorious stare. "But if you can't do that right now, I give you only this advice, son—grab her. Grab her so tight, you'll never let her go."

He lowered his head to his hands. "Hazel, you're killing me, you know that."

"Just a few words and you're free, Seth. Free to do whatever you want. Free to ruin your life if you so desire. So what is it?"

He groaned. "Kirsten is like no other." His head snapped up. His expression hardened with hidden frustration. "But because of that, I don't understand her. And so I've never been sure how to go about…well, I've never figured out how to approach—" He snuffed his last words, clearly censoring any confession.

A soft, slow, knowing smile lit on Hazel's mouth. With her gaze probing, she said, "Sometimes you just gotta wrangle 'em. You get me, son?''

He met the cattle baroness's eyes. By his expression, it seemed that want fought with logic.

At last he confessed, ''What if I wrangle her, and she just says no? Then what?''

Solemnly Hazel nodded her encouragement along with her no-nonsense advice. ''If you love her, son, and she won't have you, then you take it like a McCallum. You leave her be, but don't go running in the opposite direction. That model isn't for you, Seth. Don't fool yourself.''

Seth rubbed his eyes, his only concession to Hazel's words.

''I'm used to getting what I want, Hazel,'' he finally stated.

''Take it like a McCallum, son. State your case, bide your time and you just might be lucky enough to get what you want.''

He leaned his head back against the overly carved laminated rosewood. Several minutes ticked by as he ruminated over his choices, so many of which were beyond his control. Finally, in a fit of pique, he said, ''You know what, Hazel. I think I can handle Wall Street over Mystery.''

Hazel chuckled. ''Greenhorn,'' was all she offered.

Thirteen

———

Kirsten was in her room packing when the knock came at her door. The champagne bottle was more than half-empty and the last of her cosmetics had been tucked into her rollaway bag.

"Well, it's you," she announced, flinging the door wide-open to let Seth in.

"You act as if you were expecting me." He didn't move from the hallway. Casually he leaned on the sinuous pine baluster behind him and surveyed her.

"I wasn't 'specting you, but since you're

here, c'mon in. I want to get a few things straight.'' Her eyes read him, and she swore he smiled. It only made her madder.

''What's on your mind?'' he baited, still not entering her room.

She hugged the doorway. ''What's on my mind? Let me give you a piece of my mind,'' she offered, her expression damning. ''I, Mr. Morgan, am not the kind of woman who makes jewelry, okay?''

He looked appropriately confused. ''What are you talking about?' he asked innocently—too innocently, by her mark.

''I said,'' she repeated, narrowing her eyes, her broken heart buried deep for the moment, ''I'm not the kind of woman who makes jewelry, and I don't tolerate mistresses. We, Mr. Morgan, if we had ever married, would never have a mistress, I can assure you.''

He took a step forward.

She held up her hand to say she wasn't finished.

''Now,'' she pronounced. ''I'm quitting. So goodbye and good luck. I'm outta here. Have a good life with Nikki, and I hope you live long enough to regret it.'' She went to close the door.

He put his hand on the doorjamb.

She stared up at him.

This time he was only inches away.

"You want to talk about this, Miss Meadows?" he grunted, his eyes amused.

Disconcerted, she shook her head. "What's to talk about? I said I'd stay two weeks, and I can't. So what? Deal with it. Mary can handle all your plans. You don't need me. And if it's the pay you're worried about, hey, don't bother. I've got bigger things on the horizon. I don't need your measly paycheck, anyway."

"You sound almost bitter, Miss Meadows."

She snorted. "What gives you that idea?"

"I'd think a disenchanted employee might be a little defiant, but you sound as if there was more here. As if perhaps we were lovers and not just in a business relationship."

The unshed tears froze in her eyes.

Quietly she said, "We were lovers. I know that, at least on my end."

He uncurled his fingers from the doorjamb and entered the room.

"We are lovers, Kirsten."

Her mind tried to parry his meaning. "If you're so delusional as to think we'll continue our relationship after you're married, you need a long rest at a mental institution."

If she hadn't known better, she would have sworn he bit back a smile.

"Marriage doesn't have to exclude sex, Kirsten. I hear you can have both. It's not impossible."

"Spoken just like your father," she accused, her eyebrow rising.

"Touché," he conceded.

Smugly she continued, "Thank you very much for the mistress position, Mr. Morgan, but I'll have to decline your offer."

"Kirsten—" He tried to grab her.

She stepped away from him. The ice ball that was her heart was beginning to melt every second he was near, and she wanted him gone. She didn't want to lose control until she was out of the house and well on her way to her mother's.

"Why did you quit, anyway?" he asked, still keeping his respectful distance. "Come on, confess. It wasn't really the reason you gave, was it? When I hired you, you told me you needed this job. Then you bought your mother a house and couldn't see her going back to work until she was better—all that a fib, Miss Meadows?"

"Certainly not," she defended.

His eyes narrowed. "It looks like it, because just when things get busy over here, you decide you'd rather fling it all to the wind and work at the Mystery Diner."

Impassioned with fury, she almost struck him.

"My mother worked her tail off for Carrie and me there. And she does deserve a rest, and I'm going to give her one."

"Then stay. No one can pay you as well as I can." His gaze was riveted to hers.

She violently turned away from him. "Look, my mom may have had to waitress at the Mystery Diner, and I may have to do that, too, to keep things together. But you know what?" The tears began to melt. One slipped by, no matter how hard she tried to hold it back, and she cursed herself for it.

Damning him, she spat, "There isn't a person in Mystery who doesn't love my mom. Every customer was treated well, no matter how worn-out my mother was. And I guess that kind of stuff doesn't buy you jets and ranches, but I'd rather be loved at the Mystery Diner than live here without it."

Finished, she zipped her suitcase, picked up her half-empty bottle of champagne and stood waiting for him to move from the door so she could leave.

He didn't budge.

She lifted the champagne bottle. "Sorry about this, but I thought a celebration was in order now that I'm leaving. Just deduct it from my last paycheck."

He shrugged.

She waited.

And waited.

And waited.

Finally she dropped her suitcase on the floor with a thud.

Crossing her arms over her chest, she faced him. "Is there something more, Mr. Morgan? You look as if something's on your mind."

"Something is on my mind, Kirsten."

"And what is it?"

"Nikki," he answered, his face revealing nothing.

Angry and depressed, Kirsten had had enough. She picked up her suitcase, planning to barge right through him if necessary.

But his arms went around her and stopped her.

"Kirsten, don't leave," he whispered, a strange emotion in his eyes.

She looked at him, at his handsome face she'd grown to love, and the wound in her heart broke open. She began to weep, and quickly the tears flowed like the champagne growing flat in the bottle.

Gently he pulled her in to his chest.

She thought to fight the gesture, but there was no better place to weep than against the security of his hard chest. It was too much to resist when she was exhausted and without hope.

"Baby, don't cry," he said against her hair.

"What's not to cry about?" She sniffed, unable to get control of herself long enough to shrug off his embrace. "You won't let me leave, and the only thing on your mind is your fiancée."

He kissed her temple. "She's not my fiancée any longer. I called it off."

Maybe the champagne had really gone to her head, but for some crazy reason Kirsten thought he'd said he'd called it off.

"What?" she demanded, looking up at him.

He smiled. "I called it off. The reason she's on my mind is that I owe her a big apology—maybe even a Lamborghini. I should never have used her like I did, but Hazel said I had to settle down to keep the ranch, and I'm keeping the ranch, Kirsten. I'm not leaving Mystery."

She tried to absorb what he was saying, but none of it made sense. "I don't understand any of this. Just keep the darn ranch. What's it to Hazel or Nikki?"

Pulling her closer, he placed a tender kiss on her lips. "None of this concerns them—just you and me." His expression softened. "When I met you, Kirsten, I was convinced you were just another gold digger. It didn't bother me, because I knew all about those kinds of women. My own mother was one. You know that. So when that's all you know, that's all you expect and it doesn't bother you. Hell, I even figured I'd probably marry one of them one day just like my dad.''

Watching the emotion in his eyes go from shielded to yearning, she wondered if she was living a dream.

He continued.

"But everything you said, everything you did, went against my prejudice. Even what James said about you— I wanted to believe you were a conniving social climber, but I couldn't match up what I was thinking to what I was seeing and feeling."

Tipping her face upward, he stared down at her, a new kind of hesitation in his eyes. "Don't leave me, Kirsten. Nothing in this world will be the same if you leave me."

She let the words sink into her mind and heart. For several long moments she still couldn't believe what she was hearing, but then a new reality engulfed her, and she knew she had to be cautious.

"Seth," she whispered, her voice still deep with tears, "I can't stay here and work for you any longer whether you're married or not. It just won't work. I just can't do it.''

"What's changed?" he prodded, his tone gentle.

"I—I—" She closed her mouth and refused to say it. If she had any shred of dignity left, she had to leave without confessing her love. To do so and then find herself just another employee in the morning would kill her.

"You love me?" he asked, his stare dark and probing. "I hope so. Because I love you, Kirsten. I love you and I don't ever want another day to pass where you're not in my arms and in my bed.''

She locked gazes with him, unable to believe what she was hearing.

"Will you marry me, Kirsten?"

The words lodged in her throat where the tears had once been.

"Will you?"

"Yes," she gasped, tears springing forth anew, but this time tears of joy. "Yes, I will marry you, Seth Morgan. But not for your ranch, and not for your money." Her voice shook from the emotion. "I'll marry you because you kissed me in the cold brook, and made me feel like a woman. And lastly, I'll marry you because you're more of a man than anyone else sees. I want kindness and a warm hearth and children. Those things seem so within reach, and yet only you can bring them to me. And it will take much more than a bank account to do it.'' She laughed and wept at the same time.

Slowly his mouth crushed down on hers in a long, soul-clawing kiss that tasted of tears and champagne.

Inside she melted. Her heart leaped, but she still worried that it wasn't real, that in a moment it would all be taken away and she would wake as if in a dream.

"I love you, Kirsten, and I'm going to make you my wife if I have to sell everything and live in a shack with you and our twelve children.''

She suddenly laughed.

After those absurd words, all of a sudden she believed.

Epilogue

Hazel looked out over her beautiful Montana valley through the window of her parlor. Her face was placid, her eyes twinkling with mischief, even though Jenn Meadows's words were full of anxiety.

"It's not like her to just call me and say she's going away for a few days." Jenn nervously sipped on a hot cup of tea that Hazel had slipped some whiskey into.

"She's an adult, dear. She has a right to take a few days off." Hazel sat down next to her. "Besides, maybe that boss of hers sent her on an errand to Paris, or such."

Jenn shook her head. "No, she'd tell me. Besides—" her face took on a more troubled cast "—I think there's something going on with that boss of hers. She hasn't said anything, but I do hope they're not fooling around with each other." Her eyes darkened. "I'd hate for her to have to go through what I've gone through—"

"And that reminds me, dear. Have you met Jim, Seth's ranch manager? I know the girls have really enjoyed riding up there. Why don't we have him plan one of those old-fashioned hayrides for us? We'll take along a little supper and have a picnic right by the mill."

Kirsten's mother rolled her eyes. "I've heard all the town gossip on how you like to play matchmaker, and I can't even begin to imagine you'd be up to those old tricks with me, Hazel. I'm too old and too ugly."

"You're a beauty, my dear, and there's no such thing as too old for romance. Besides, this isn't some kind of scheme of mine. Jim's a fine man. Lost his wife to cancer four years ago. Never remarried and never even thought about it, I assure you."

Jenn sighed. "A hayride sounds like great fun, Hazel, but all of this is beside the point. I just can't get it out of my head that something's going on with Kirsten—"

"Who's coming, Ebby?" Hazel asked, her sixth sense picking up on visitors even before the dust of the vehicle could be seen in the distance.

"I don't know," Hazel's housekeeper mused, going to the window. After a few moments she said, "Looks like a Jeep. I think it might be Seth Morgan's Jeep. Yep, looks like his, all right."

"Maybe it's Kirsten," Jenn announced, going to the window.

Sure enough, the Jeep came to a halt and Seth jumped out of the vehicle. He went around to the passenger side to help Kirsten out.

"Something's different. I can see that from here," Jenn mused, her forehead furrowed— now not with fear, but rather curious expectation.

Ebby went to the front door and opened it.

Quickly the couple was inside, with Jenn admonishing her daughter.

"Kirsten, I know you're an adult and all, but really, I just want a phone number, anything, if you decide to take off like that. What if something happened?" she said, giving her daughter a hug.

Seth cleared his throat, but didn't intrude.

"I've something to tell you," Kirsten said, looking at her mother and Hazel.

"Should we sit down?" Jenn asked, caution all over her beautiful face.

"Nonsense," Hazel huffed. "Can't you see that sparkler on her finger, Jenn? Your daughter's gone run off and got herself married."

Jenn's gaze fell to Kirsten's left ring finger. There was a pink-lavender diamond surrounded by two others on a thin platinum band.

"Kirsten?" Jenn gasped. "Oh, Kirsten." She hugged her laughing daughter.

When they parted, she added, "But you should have told us. Carrie will be beside herself that she missed you getting married."

Kirsten sat them all down, her hand locked with Seth's as she took her place next to him. "We wanted to tell you, but it was very sudden. And when Seth decides something, come hell or high water, it's going to happen."

"When did you both decide this? I didn't even know you had a romance," Jenn commented. She turned to her new son-in-law. "And I thought you were engaged already to some woman in New York City."

Seth released a wry grin. "Entirely my mistake. Because when I took one look at Kirsten, I knew she was the one I wanted and no other would do." He squeezed his bride's hand. "And once I got her convinced that I loved her and this was forever, we saw no reason to make a circus of it like Nikki'd been doing. We flew to Greece and got married shipboard.''

"But we're going to have a small ceremony here,'' Kirsten added hastily. "Because I do want Carrie to be my maid of honor.'' She leaned over and took her mother's hand. "And I want you to be the second woman at the reception to dance with your new son-in-law, Mom.''

It took a few moments for Jenn to absorb all that was being explained to her.

But finally, when she had regained herself, she stood and gave Seth a big hug. "Welcome to the family, Seth,'' Jenn said.

He gave her a big bear hug. "I'm honored, Jenn. You three make the best family I've ever seen.''

Jenn smiled. "We all love each other. That's all a family needs, right, Kirsten?''

"That's all you need,'' Kirsten agreed, looking at her husband with love-filled eyes.

"Now that that's settled,'' Hazel interjected, "when are the babies coming along? No sense in wasting time. You've both seen the world. I say settle down and get to doing what God put you in this green valley for.''

Seth laughed. "Hazel, you're too much.'' He

looked at his bride and said, "Should you tell them or should I?"

Kirsten shrugged helplessly. She faced the other two women and said, "We don't have it completely confirmed, but let's just say don't be surprised if the baby comes along sooner than later."

Tears glistened in Jenn's eyes. "How amazing. All of this. How wonderful," she uttered, beside herself.

Kirsten went to be by her side.

But Hazel was on to the next challenge.

"We've got to have a couple of parties celebrating this here thing," she announced, mostly to Ebby, who was in the background making notes on all that had transpired.

"We don't need much, Hazel," Seth added.

"Not much! You're talking Mystery people here. We need to pull out all the stops!" Hazel admonished.

Her eyes twinkled. "And the first thing we should do is go on a hayride! Doesn't that sound like fun? We could pack a nice supper and Jim—he works for you, Seth, I believe—why, he could take the whole family here for a celebration."

Jenn recovered from her happy shock just long enough to say to Hazel, "Hey, I know what you're doing—'' before Seth and Kirsten and Ebby interrupted, each with their own contributions to the idea of a hayride.

In the ensuing fracas, Hazel returned to look out her parlor window.

Mystery Valley lay like a blanket of emerald moss beneath the majestic snow-covered peaks of the mountains. The sun was sinking, painting Mount Mystery a ruby-red. In the far distance a stag was chasing a doe across the golden fields. The cattle munched peaceably, their fat bodies casting long, lazy shadows across the hay fields.

"You can count another happy couple off your matchmaking list, you sly girl," Ebby said, standing next to her boss in the window. "So are you resting on your laurels?"

The cattle baroness put that thought to rest. "Certainly not," she said.

"So what are you thinking now, Hazel?" Ebby asked above the excited din.

Hazel couldn't repress the twinkle in her Prussian-blue eyes.

The only thing she said was, "Next!"

* * * * *

Don't miss the latest miniseries from award-winning author Marie Ferrarella:

The MOM SQUAD

Meet...

Sherry Campbell—ambitious newswoman who makes headlines when a handsome billionaire arrives to sweep her off her feet...and shepherd her new son into the world!
**A BILLIONAIRE AND A BABY, SE#1528,
available March 2003**

Joanna Prescott—Nine months after her visit to the sperm bank, her old love rescues her from a burning house—then delivers her baby....
**A BACHELOR AND A BABY, SD#1503,
available April 2003**

Chris "C.J." Jones—FBI agent, expectant mother and always on the case. When the baby comes, will her irresistible partner be by her side?
THE BABY MISSION, IM#1220, available May 2003

Lori O'Neill—A forbidden attraction blows down this pregnant Lamaze teacher's tough-woman facade and makes her consider the love of a lifetime!
**BEAUTY AND THE BABY, SR#1668,
available June 2003**

The Mom Squad—these single mothers-to-be are ready for labor...and true love!

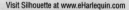

COMING NEXT MONTH

#1507 WHERE THERE'S SMOKE…—Barbara McCauley
Dynasties: The Barones
Emily Barone couldn't remember anything—except for the fireman who'd saved her life. Soft-spoken and innocent, she had no defenses against Shane Cummings's bone-melting charm. Before she knew it, she'd given him her body and her heart. But would she trade her Barone riches to find happily-ever-after with her real-life hero?

#1508 THE GENTRYS: CINCO—Linda Conrad
The Gentrys
The last thing rancher Cinco Gentry needed was a beautiful, headstrong retired air force captain disrupting his well-ordered life. But when a crazed killer threatened Meredith Powell, Cinco agreed to let her stay with him. And though Meredith's independent ways continually clashed with his protective streak, Cinco realized he, too, was in danger—of falling for his feisty houseguest!

#1509 CHEROKEE BABY—Sheri WhiteFeather
A whirlwind affair had left Julianne McKenzie with one giant surprise…. She was pregnant with ranch owner Bobby Elk's baby. The sexy Cherokee was not in the market for marriage but, once he learned Julianne carried his child, he quickly offered her a permanent place in his life. Yet Julianne would only settle for *all* of her Cherokee lover's heart.

#1510 SLEEPING WITH BEAUTY—Laura Wright
Living alone in the Colorado Rockies, U.S. Marshal Dan Mason didn't want company, especially of the drop-dead-gorgeous variety. But when a hiking accident left violet-eyed "Angel" on his doorstep with no memory and no identity, he took her in. Dan had closed off his heart years ago—could this mysterious beauty bring him back to life?

#1511 THE COWBOY'S BABY BARGAIN—Emilie Rose
The Baby Bank
Brooke Blake's biological clock was ticking, so she struck an irresistible bargain with tantalizing cowboy Caleb Lander. The deal? She'd give him back his family's land if he fathered her baby! But Brooke had no inkling that their arrangement would be quite so pleasurable, and she ached to keep this heartstoppingly handsome rancher in her bed and in her life.

#1512 HER CONVENIENT MILLIONAIRE—Gail Dayton
Desperate to escape an arranged marriage, Sherry Nyland needed a temporary husband—fast! Millionaire Micah Scott could never resist a damsel in distress, so when Sherry proposed a paper marriage, he agreed to help her. But it wasn't long before Micah was falling for his lovely young bride. Now he just had to convince Sherry that he intended to love, honor and cherish her…forever!